WILL
BE BLESSED!

Bill J——

THE REVENGE OF THE TIMBER WOLF

The Blood Warrior Trilogy

©2014 William H. Joiner, Jr.

Edited by Missy Brewer

Book design by Michael Campbell, MCWriting.com

Cover design by Bryan Gehrke, MyCoverDesigner.com

ISBN: 978-1503178625

For more information visit www.williamjoinerauthor.com

THE REVENGE OF THE
TIMBER WOLF

The Blood Warrior Trilogy

WILLIAM H. JOINER, JR.

CONTENTS

Midnight Hunt 1

The Birth of Blood Warrior. . . . 5

Family to Feed 11

Learning to Hunt 17

Friends and Enemies Above 25

Dark Demon 31

Glutton 37

Sly Cougar 45

Red Fang 49

Battle of Thunder 59

Tasha 63

Dolt 67

Blood Warrior Returns 75

It Begins 81

Facing Talon 85

Sly's Turn 89

Destroying Demon 93

Red Fang Revenge 99

Rage and Reprisal 105

Barky Meets His Match 111

Thinning the Pack 119

The Healing 127

The Fathers 131

The Final Hunt 135

The Dark Battle 145

Finding Tasha 151

Hawk's Helper 155

Red Fang Invades 161

New Families 165

The Betrayal 171

The Final Revenge 175

Acknowledgements 181

MIDNIGHT HUNT

A full silver moon dominated the cloudless night sky with its thousands of blinking stars. The peaceful tranquility was shattered by the chilling howl of a wolf. The wolf didn't finish his howl before he was joined by a symphony of howling wolves that pricked the ears of every moose, elk, deer and prey animal within earshot. A wolf pack on the hunt was a matter of grave concern to all of them.

The howling stopped suddenly, punctuated by sharp barks and yips. The silence that followed was pregnant with a heavy foreboding. The quiet was eerie. The animals could hear themselves breathe.

When the large elk smelled the first faint trace of the approaching wolf pack, he bolted. The reddish-tan bull had enormous antlers that trailed down his back as he ran. The elk flattened all the smaller shinnery and brush that was in his way as he dashed for survival. The whites of his eyes were reflected by the light of the moon. As he ran, he twisted his head, looking for the wolves.

Thunder was the leader and largest member of the pack. His superior speed quickly separated him from the rest of the pack. He was rapidly closing the distance between the hunter and the hunted. Thunder vaulted onto the elk's hindquarters and fastened his sharp teeth to one of its hamstrings. Thunder clamped down with all the strength in his powerful jaws as he felt the flesh give way, severing the hamstring. The terrified animal was now running on three legs. The elk kicked, trying to dislodge the wolf, but Thunder desperately hung on. He knew the bull's hooves could be deadly if the elk connected with one of his kicks.

Despite being reduced to being a tripod, the bull still managed to buck off the wolf. When Thunder hit the ground, he immediately rolled and came to his feet. The elk lowered his head, snorted and charged the wolf, attempting to gore him with the sharp points of his antlers.

While Thunder was large for a timber wolf, he was also blessed with great quickness. He narrowly avoided the bull's antlers, loudly barking to his pack, "Here! We're over here!"

When the rest of the pack arrived, Thunder and one of the others latched onto the elk's throat while the rest ripped at the belly of their immobilized prey. The six wolves pulled the elk down and began feasting. Thunder threw his head back and howled, "Thank you, Father Wolf in the Sky, for providing for us!"

Thunder's pack of timber wolves roamed what would be known centuries later as Yellowstone National Park. Their territory was mostly modern-day Wyoming but extended into

Montana and Idaho, consisting of vast woodlands and grass-lands. The land teemed with wildlife of every species. The rivers and lakes were choked with fish. It was a great time to be a wolf.

THE BIRTH
OF BLOOD
WARRIOR

The next morning, Shadow, who was the matriarch of the pack, began frantically digging in the soft earth and leaves on the forest floor, slinging a steady spray of dirt behind her. Shadow was surrounded by lodgepole pines and quaking aspen. The green needles of the pine made a sharp contrast to the white bark of the aspen. The sun shone brightly in the clear blue sky. The temperatures in the spring month of March were chilly at dawn, warming up at midday. The harshest part of the winter was over but there were still substantial patches of snow on the ground.

Shadow was a beautiful silver timber wolf. Her body told her that it was time to prepare a den for the birth of her pups. When the digging was done and the den completed, Shadow felt a comfort in the confined space and the smell of the damp earth. The litter of wolf pups was born when Shadow was safe in the underground den. When the first pup was born, Shadow murmured as she licked him clean, "Oh my, aren't you a big strong son. You have such beautiful gray fur. I will call you Zev." The second pup was a gray female. Shadow exclaimed, "I am blessed with a little daughter. Your name will be Nashoba." Shadow grunted as the third pup passed from her body, "Another son! I love your brown fur. It matches the earth. You look like you have been digging in the ground. That will be your name, Digger." The fourth pup was an easy birth. Shadow glowed, "Thank you, Father Wolf. I am doubly blessed with another daughter. Sweetheart, you will be known as Otsandra."

Wolf pups are born blind and deaf. They open their eyes at two weeks and begin to hear at three weeks. As Shadow began to lick and clean her pups, they instinctively began to squirm and mew, blindly searching for her teats. Shadow allowed them to nurse but knew that there was still one more pup to be born.

The last pup was twice the size of the other pups, causing Shadow to flinch in pain. With one final long strain, the last pup slipped from her body. When she examined him, Shadow was stunned. "My son, you are huge! Your fur is blacker than the darkest night!"

All five pups suckled her rich milk until their bellies pooched out. As they slept, Shadow emerged at the den's entrance, stretching her long legs and arching her back. She was cramping from being confined for so long. Shadow also basked in the warm rays of the midday sun. The sight and the trilling song from a yellow-breasted meadowlark made her smile.

Her mate was Thunder, a huge, physically imposing gray timber wolf. He had been standing guard at the den's entrance. Thunder sniffed her and softly barked, "Shadow, how are you? How are the pups?"

Shadow replied, "I am a little tired, but we have five beautiful pups—three males and two females. But Thunder—one of the pups is different."

Thunder nuzzled her silver fur and said, "Different how?"

Shadow licked Thunder's jaw, "One of the male pups is the biggest that I've ever given birth to but there is just something different about him. His fur is the blackest I've ever seen on a wolf, but it's more than that. He's just—different."

Thunder threw back his head triumphantly and howled, "I have five new children, including three strong boys. One of my sons has been touched by Father Wolf!"

Shadow joined his howl. "Thank you, Father Wolf in the Sky! Thank you for my new children!"

Shadow continued, "I have named the other pups but I do not have a name for the big black pup. I think you should name him."

That night Thunder had a dream about his new son. In the dream, he saw the pup grow to be a mighty warrior. His son was surrounded by blood but it was not his. It was the blood of his enemies. Thunder awoke from the dream with a start. He nudged the sleeping Shadow awake. "Father Wolf has spoken to me about the name for our son. He is to be called Blood Warrior." Shadow wagged her tail in agreement.

Wolves use scent to communicate by marking their territory with urine or scat. This marking tells other wolves to stay out. Wolves also rely on scent to tell when a female is ready to breed. They are very social animals and converse with barks, whines, yips and howls. Howling is what other animals hear the most, and is used to locate other wolves and to praise the Father Wolf in the Sky.

At two weeks, the pups opened their eyes. Shadow softly barked to Blood Warrior, "Your eyes—I can't get over your eyes. Your golden eyes shine like the sun!" The other four pups had the traditional blue eyes, standard for wolf pups. A wolf pup's blue eyes normally fade to yellow or brown when becoming an adult. Shadow also praised the other pups for their beautiful eyes.

After feeding them, Shadow emerged from her den and excitedly announced to the pack, "The pups' eyes are open! Four of them have beautiful blue eyes and Blood Warrior has eyes that glow like twin golden suns!"

After a month, the pups came out of the den to join the rest of the pack. Wolf packs consist of offspring from the alpha male and his mate. The alpha male and his mate are the only members in the pack that are allowed to breed. Most wolves, when they come of breeding age, generally leave their pack to select a mate and begin their own pack. Wolves are usually sexually mature by two years of age.

The five new pups dashed around and frolicked on wobbly legs. They were greeted with much licking by their father Thunder, their older brothers Raul and Ulrich, and their older sisters Aiyana, Larentia and Landga. Raul, Ulrich, Larentia and Landga had the traditional gray coats, while Aiyana had dark red fur.

Their sisters gushed over all the pups. Aiyana mewed between licks, "Aww, you are just adorable!"

Larentia gushed over Blood Warrior, "What beautiful black fur! And look at those golden eyes!"

Landga licked each pup, saying, "I love the smell of new puppies!" Raul and Ulrich licked the pups too but didn't fawn over them as their sisters did because their dignity wouldn't allow it.

FAMILY
TO FEED

Thunder crept through the forest as he began his daily hunt. His nose wrinkled as he smelled the tantalizing aroma of deer. The smell made him start to salivate, thinking about the deer's delicious flesh and nourishing blood. Thunder always hunted into the wind to take advantage of his sharpest sense, his sense of smell. He had excellent eyesight and hearing, but his nose provided him with the most information.

Thunder was distracted from his search for game for a scant second as a brilliantly colored bluebird flitted through the air just above his head.

Thunder found the deer by following her scent. She was grazing on tender green shoots of timber oatgrass in a small opening in the trees. Later in the summer the oatgrass would turn brown but still be full of nutrients. He soundlessly approached her until he was close enough to rush in for the kill.

The doe smelled the wolf before she saw him and immediately took flight. She bounded away with her tail flagging but only covered ten yards before she was bowled over by the big wolf. Thunder savagely ripped her throat out as she bleated and kicked. He began feeding as she was dying. The hot blood of the deer was an elixir to the wolf. Powerful bites from his massive jaws crushed the doe's bones.

Thunder brought the freshly killed deer back to the den. Even though the big doe weighed over 100 pounds, the muscular Thunder carried it with ease. Since he had already fed on the deer, its hair was blood-soaked and its entrails dangled from its open belly.

Shadow was the first to eat as befitting her place in the pack. She thrust her muzzle into the deer's belly, ripping out chunks of flesh and intestines. As Shadow gulped the meat down, she sighed with a satisfied growl, "Ahhh, this tastes so good! I was starving for fresh deer meat and blood!"

After Shadow ate her fill, she and Thunder lay down together and watched their happy pack eat and play with great satisfaction. Shadow tenderly barked, "It is days like this that make being a wolf so glorious. I love my family."

The pecking order for feeding for a wolf pack begins with the alpha male and female first, followed by the older pack members next. The youngest always eats last. The only exception is when there are newborn pups. The five pups began to feed immediately. Every day, the pups suckled less and less from Shadow and began eating meat more and more.

The days lengthened into summer. The wolf family spent as much time playing and romping with each other as they did hunting. The new pups would jump on each other with play-growls. Stalking each other in play laid the foundation for hunting skills that would eventually be needed for survival.

There was one disruption in the play of the pups. Zev, Digger, Nashoba and Otsandra ran away yipping in terror whenever they saw Blood Warrior bounding in their direction to play. Blood Warrior didn't realize he was twice as big and three times as strong as his litter-mates. He just wanted to play, but his attempt at play resulted in his brothers and sisters cartwheeling across the green grass as he accidentally ran over them. Finally, Shadow would intervene by grabbing Blood Warrior by the scruff of his neck and gently shaking him as she laughed, "Settle down, you big brute. You are killing your brothers and sisters with love."

Thunder loved all his children, but Shadow could see a unique pride shine in his eyes when he looked at their son with shining black fur and glistening golden eyes. Blood Warrior was a natural leader. He was assertive and outspoken. Even at a young age, Blood Warrior bowed to Thunder's authority, but to no else's—not even Shadow's. None of the other pack members resented or challenged him on this. They all recognized that Blood Warrior was born to lead.

Each of the pack members developed special bonds with each other. As with any family, some personalities fit together better than others.

Aiyana was thoughtful and kind, usually thinking of others before herself. She was a caregiver. She liked nothing better than caring for the puppies. If one of the pups yipped in pain,

Aiyana sometimes even beat Shadow to tend to the pup's hurt.

While Zev was fun loving and carefree as most puppies are, he sometimes pushed the limits of fun. His favorite prank was to catch the other wolves asleep and nip their tails. When they awoke with a growl, Zev would scurry back to the protective refuge of Aiyana.

Zev played this prank on Blood Warrior only one time. Zev silently stalked the dozing Blood Warrior. When Zev nipped his tail, Blood Warrior sprang to his feet with a fierce growl. This startled Zev so badly he fell over backward from the shock. Blood Warrior, seeing that it was Zev, laughingly barked, "Hey, little brother, you are always so funny! I love to play with you!"

Zev quickly got back to his feet and sprinted in the direction of Aiyana, yipping as he went, "Nooo big brother! I don't want to play!"

Blood Warrior laughed even louder with delight. A chase made it be even more fun! Blood Warrior began the pursuit of Zev, playfully threatening, "Here I come Zevie! I'm going to get you!"

Aiyana saw Zev in a mad dash coming at her, with Blood Warrior not far behind. Aiyana thought, *Oh, wolf shit! This is not going to end well.* As he got to her, Zev dived under her belly to put her between him and the charging Blood Warrior. By then, Blood Warrior had built up too big a head of steam. Aiyana yelled to no avail, "Stoooppp!!" Blood Warrior tried to put on the brakes but bowled over Aiyana and Zev.

The downed pair were both momentarily stunned. As they slowly staggered to their feet, Blood Warrior apologetically began licking them, "I'm sorry! I'm sorry!" Zev learned that a playful Blood Warrior could still inadvertently hurt you.

Zev attached himself to Aiyana always being at her heels. Zev even snuggled up to her to sleep. Aiyana, in turn, doted on Zev. She licked and pampered all the pups but gave Zev special attention. Whenever a kill was brought back to the pack, Aiyana always made sure that Zev had plenty to eat before she ate herself.

Zev loved all his family members but he had a special place in his heart for Aiyana, even over his mother, Shadow. Zev wagged his tail the hardest whenever he saw Aiyana return from a hunt. Because they shared such a deep love for each other, Aiyana took it upon herself to teach Zev to hunt. For an older wolf to teach a younger one to hunt requires a special bond. Normally, the father or the mother taught their young to hunt. For Aiyana to take on that role showed how unique her relationship was with Zev.

Larentia and Landga were inseparable. Where you saw one, you saw the other. Larentia was impatient and a risk taker. Rules chafed her. She had no problem bending or even breaking the rules given by Thunder even though Thunder's rules were made to keep the members of the pack safe. She didn't care. Larentia wanted what she wanted, when she wanted it, the rules be damned.

On the other hand Landga was a follower. She tended to be quiet and liked to please the other wolves. Because of their opposite personalities, she and Larentia rarely argued. This compatibility made them perfect companions and hunting partners.

Once when they were out on a hunt, Landga warned, "Sister, we are going farther than Father told us to go. Thunder said for us to stay within the boundaries he gave us. Father said that he didn't want us to go out too far in case we need help. He wants to be able to come to our aid quickly."

Larentia sighed, "Oh Landga, you are as big a worrywart as Father! Nothing is going to happen to us. We will be fine. You need to loosen up and have a little fun!" Larentia continued the hunt without a care in the world. Landga, loyally, stuck with her sister but still had an uneasy feeling about breaking her father's rules.

LEARNING TO HUNT

R aul was a lone wolf. He didn't particularly crave the company of the other pack members. Most of the time he hunted by himself. Raul was independent, serious, quiet and responsible. Thunder could always count on him to do his part for the family. Raul's greatest pride was to bring a kill that he had hunted and killed by himself back to the pack.

Thunder cautioned Raul, "Son, I know you can take care of yourself. You are grown and I won't put any restrictions on you. But, you need to be aware that hunting by yourself carries additional danger. Please consider taking me or one of your sisters or your brother with you when you hunt."

Raul nodded his head, "I will try to do that, Father." Raul did not intend to lie to his father but the allure to hunt by himself was just too strong. He maintained his solitary hunting style.

One day while hunting, Raul smelled and trailed a large bull moose. When he saw the size of it, Raul thought, *Father would not want me to try to take this big beast down by myself. But think what kind of hero I would be to my family if I killed him and brought them all here for a feast!* Raul fearlessly stalked and attacked the huge moose. He burst out of the thick shinnery and latched on to the hamstring of one of the moose's giant legs.

The moose grunted as he fled in panic with the timber wolf hitchhiking on one leg. The big bull did not concern himself about any obstacles. He knocked down almost anything that was in the way of his stampede except for the largest of the trees. In the meantime, Raul was being pummeled by the remnants of the trees and brush that the moose was plowing through. One medium-sized aspen scraped down the moose's side and knocked Raul completely off his prey.

Raul laid on the forest floor as he heard the moose continue to crash through the woods. The tree had hit Raul with such force that he wasn't quite sure if he was dead or alive. He lifted one eyelid, then tested the other one. Raul thought, *I seem to be alive.* He gingerly got to his feet. As he limped off, he thought, *Oh great, now what am I going to tell Father when he asks me what happened to me and why am I limping? Maybe he won't notice. Oh wolf shit, who am I kidding? Father notices everything. I will probably get the biggest lecture I've ever gotten.* Raul was right. The lecture from Thunder was lengthy.

Ulrich was aloof but not as standoffish as Raul. Unlike his brother, he rarely hunted alone. Most of the time he teamed up with Aiyana. Ulrich thought Aiyana needed his protection and he wanted to keep her safe. When they hunted together, Ulrich always prefaced the hunt, "Aiyana, stay behind me. If we find something, I will take the lead on the kill."

This always exasperated Aiyana. "Father Wolf, Ulrich! Will you give it a rest? I am perfectly capable of killing a deer, elk or even a small moose. I am what's known in the forest as a *wolf*! That's what *wolves* do!" Ulrich ignored her protests and continued to try to safeguard her.

Ulrich and Aiyana began stalking a cow elk. As usual, Ulrich was a body length in front of Aiyana. When they got in position, Ulrich muttered in a barely audible whisper, "On three: one… two…" At the count of two, Aiyana prematurely burst past him to charge the elk. The frightened elk sped away, exposing her vulnerable hamstrings and underbelly. Aiyana's sharp teeth ripped a hole in the elk's belly, causing intestines to spill from the gash. The elk kicked at the wolf in an attempt to kill her. One of the cow's hooves clipped the side of Aiyana's skull, knocking her unconscious.

As Aiyana began to regain consciousness, the first thing she saw was Ulrich standing over her. Ulrich whined as he licked her, "Thank Father Wolf, you're alive! Don't ever do that again! This is exactly why I should be the lead on a kill. I am bigger and stronger than you!"

Aiyana slowly got to her feet. She could see the dead elk piled up in a heap just the other side of a clearing. Irritated that she knew Ulrich was right, she snapped, "Wolf shit! Now I guess I'm never going to hear the end of this! Just shut up and let's eat."

Digger always looked like he had been digging in the dirt. In addition, he always appeared a little disheveled. Most of the other wolves were fastidious about licking themselves clean after a kill. Not Digger. You could see pieces of what he had to eat for the last week on the ends of the hairs on his coat.

Shadow chided him, "Tell me, son. Are you never hungry enough to finish feeding?"

Digger knew she was referencing the food remnants on his fur. "C'mon Mother, I'll get it cleaned up in a minute. I've been busy." Shadow shook her head as she knew that Digger would never find that minute to clean himself completely.

Nashoba had a good heart but she was easily distracted. It was hard for her to stay focused on a task for long. When Shadow was starting to teach her how to hunt, Nashoba broke their concealment on a deer stalk to suddenly chase a butterfly. Shadow called after her, "Nashoba, what are you doing? We were stalking a deer here, remember? Now, the deer is gone! Do you think a butterfly is more filling then a deer?"

Nashoba sheepishly replied, "Sorry Mother, but did you see the colors on that butterfly?"

Shadow wearily shook her head, "You are going to starve to death if something happens to us! I am trying to teach you how to hunt! Please pay attention!"

Nashoba hung her head. "I promise I will do better." Shadow sighed as she wondered if her daughter would really pay closer attention.

Otsandra loved to observe. Sometimes when the other puppies frolicked and played, Otsandra would just stand or sit and watch. She was entertained by watching the other wolves, or the birds chirping and singing in the trees. Otsandra was also a dreamer. She loved to lay down in the shade on a warm day and daydream about the pack she was going to have one day. Otsandra longed to be an alpha female and have large litters of puppies every year. She imagined her mate would be the biggest and strongest of all the wolves.

When Shadow would catch Otsandra daydreaming, she would ask, "Daughter, what are you thinking about?"

Otsandra would always respond with the same answer, "Mother, I'm thinking about how I want one day to be just like you." The daughter would then affectionately lick and nuzzle her mother.

Despite his personal hygiene, Digger was an excellent hunter. One day he announced to Nashoba and Otsandra, "Sisters, I want you to be part of my hunting party." The female wolves danced and wagged their tails in their excitement of being chosen by their brother. Up until that point, they had assumed they would be hunting by themselves as the rest of the pack had already chosen their hunting partners.

Impulsively they began to lick Digger. Nashoba scrunched her face in a look of disgust as she tried to wipe her tongue off on her own fur. "That's disgusting! What is that on your fur?" Otsandra was too busy gagging to say anything.

Digger proudly responded, "That's some of that elk I killed last week! Hunting with me will allow you two to feast to your heart's content!"

What they didn't know was that Thunder had strongly suggested to Digger that he take his sisters with him. Thunder had said privately to Digger, "I want Nashoba and Otsandra to hunt with you. I would feel better about their safety if you were there. You would be good for them and maybe they could inspire you to keep yourself clean!"

Digger lowered his head and sheepishly dug a paw in the dirt. "Awww Father, I will clean my fur as soon as I get a minute."

As they prepared for their first hunt, Digger gave his sisters instructions. "Girls, I have heard about how you hunt and there has to be some changes. Nashoba, I'm going to need you to concentrate more. No chasing butterflies in the middle of a hunt!" Nashoba giggled at the thought of Digger's reaction if she took off after a butterfly. Digger continued, "Otsandra, you are going to have to be more aggressive. You can't just sit back and watch us hunt. To have a healthy pack, everybody has to do their job."

Both females wagged their tails and said in unison, "We will, brother! We promise!" They looked at each other, delighted they had said the same thing at the same time. They began to giggle uncontrollably. Digger shook his head and thought, *Father Wolf, I'm going to need your help with these two.*

With Digger taking the lead, the three wolves slowing stalked a buck deer. Digger softly said to Nashoba, "Circle around the deer until you are on the opposite side. Otsandra and I will lay down here. I want you to rush him. Try to spook him in our direction. We will be waiting in ambush."

Nashoba crept backwards until she could safely make a wide circle to get behind the buck. As she slipped up on their prey, she looked for her brother and sister but could not see them. She knew where they were but they were so well concealed they weren't visible.

With a growl, Nashoba charged the buck, attempting to herd it towards the hidden wolves. In a panic-fueled flight, the deer fled in the direction of Digger and Otsandra. While attempting to evade Nashoba, the frightened buck was surprised by a wolf who seemed to rise up out of the ground.

Digger snarled and locked his teeth on the deer's throat. Otsandra just stared at the fascinating struggle of life and death for the deer. The buck was thrashing wildly as Digger desperately held on. When the pursuing Nashoba arrived, she barked loudly at Otsandra, "Sister, HELP!"

Nashoba began slashing at the deer's belly with her fangs. Otsandra woke from her trance and tore at one of the deer's hamstrings. With the trio of wolves in full attack mode, the deer quickly died.

With the fallen trophy at their feet, the wolves all joined in a chorus of victorious howls. The rest of the pack were within earshot and loped toward the kill. After everyone had eaten their fill, Digger barked, "Nashoba and Otsandra, you did a great job!" Digger stretched the truth a little bit, "I couldn't have done this without you." The rest of the pack licked the female wolves in gratitude. None of them licked Digger for obvious reasons.

As both sisters swaggered, Nashoba rambunctiously barked, "While Digger held the buck, I attacked his belly!"

Otsandra didn't mention her late start but proudly responded, "And, I cut one of his hamstrings!" The rest of their pack rained compliments on them. After that day, the two sisters were changed wolves. They were all business when it came time to hunt.

Later, in a private moment, Thunder said to Digger, "I'm proud of you, son."

Shadow added, "I can't believe what you've done with your sisters! You not only kept them safe but you taught them something valuable at the same time." Digger said nothing but beamed with pride at the praise of his father and mother.

FRIENDS AND ENEMIES ABOVE

B arky was a flying squirrel. He came by his name honestly. The aptly named Barky would not shut up. His coat was dark brown, almost black, while his face was framed by soft gray fur. His eyes were a light orange. From the safety of a tree or his den in the hollow of a tree, Barky threatened and harassed every living creature within sight. Because he was a flying (a more accurate description would be gliding) squirrel, he had half a dozen dens scattered throughout the forest, all strategically placed to provide a quick escape from danger. He needed them all, as his small body could not back up his big mouth.

Barky tried to provoke Thunder. "Oh my, it's the great Thunder! Am I supposed to be shaking with fear?"

Barky's trash-talking didn't have the desired effect as Thunder laughed, "No, you definitely should not be afraid of me! If I was starving to death, I wouldn't eat you. I'm sure your meat would kill me all by itself!"

This made Barky laugh. "Don't be badmouthing the taste of my flesh! I would probably be the finest meal you ever had!"

All the wolves in Thunder's pack got a kick out of Barky, none more so than Blood Warrior. Barky chattered to the young wolf, "What the hell are you? You look like some overgrown coyote! Hey coyote, are you from around here?"

Blood Warrior convulsed in laughter. When he caught his breath, he barked, "Thank you, Father Wolf in the Sky! I never thought I'd ever see a talking snack!" Now it was Barky's turn to laugh. Blood Warrior continued, "I bet I'm the only wolf who's ever seen a bear turd climb a tree and speak!" That first exchange began a lifelong friendship between the wolf and the squirrel.

One day, after the litter of young pups was a few months old, Thunder and Shadow went off hunting together. The rest of the pack was teamed up and were also hunting as it required several kills of large prey per week to keep the pack well and healthy. They hunted deer, elk and moose, although they would kill and eat any available small animal, bird or reptile. Aiyana was the only adult wolf left to guard the litter.

The majestic golden eagle slowly circling overhead was Talon. He had a wingspan of over eight feet. Talon had golden-brown plumage with powerful claws that provided a vise-like grip to capture his prey. He would plunge from thousands of feet in the air in a dive approaching 200 miles per hour, braking at the last minute to strike his unsuspecting victim. Talon would rip big chunks of flesh from his kill with his strong, formidable beak, usually eating the hapless victim alive. He mostly fed on small mammals and birds but he had a particular fondness for wolf pups. There was just something special about the taste of meat from a fellow predator, and he liked the idea of eliminating competition for his food.

Talon was cruising the gray overcast sky when he spotted the pups frolicking in a green patch of fescue under Aiyana's watchful eye. Since she was focused on the pups, Aiyana did not see the eagle soaring at an altitude where he was only a small speck. The only thing of note to catch her attention from above were two mourning doves roosting on the limb of a nearby aspen. The doves relaxed her senses further, their soft cooing completing the tranquil scene.

Talon folded his wings and began a power dive. Before Aiyana knew what was happening, Zev yelped as Talon buried his claws deep into Zev's small body. With a mighty flapping of his wings, Talon was trying to become airborne, carrying his prize. Aiyana launched herself at the great eagle. She bit down on the leg whose claw clutched Zev. At first she thought she was going to be able to make the eagle drop Zev as Talon tried to shake her off.

Talon made a strategic move by grabbing at one of the other pups milling around in confusion with his other claw, shrieking, "I'm going to kill all these pups!"

In fear for the safety of the other pups, Aiyana turned his leg loose and screamed at the other four pups, "Quick! Get in the den! Get in the den!" Three of the pups ran for the den as fast as their little legs could carry them. The only one who didn't run was Blood Warrior. He stood his ground, growling, the fur on the back of his neck bristling at the golden eagle. Aiyana nipped him hard, "Get moving, I said! Now!!"

When Blood Warrior disappeared down the mouth of the den, Aiyana turned back to continue her fight with Talon, but it was too late. Talon was disappearing out of sight with the squirming Zev tightly gripped in his claws. Zev weakly mewed, "Help me, Aiyana... help me... help... hel..."

As he flew away, Talon shrieked to Aiyana, "Tell Thunder, thanks for the meal!"

Aiyana screamed, "Zev! Zev! My poor Zevie!" Aiyana began howling but it was also part screeching and keening as she was overcome with the pain and grief at the loss of her beloved Zev.

Off in the distance, Thunder, Shadow and the rest of the pack heard her howls. They could tell something was desperately wrong. Every wolf immediately stopped what they were doing and sprinted back to the den. Thunder was the first to arrive. Aiyana was prostrate on the ground, yipping hysterically.

Thunder grabbed her by the scruff of her neck and shook her, "Aiyana, stop that! Tell me what has happened!"

She sobbed, "The eagle got Zev! It's all my fault. I was supposed to protect him and I didn't do my job."

Thunder knew exactly which eagle she was talking about. He and Talon had a previous run-in when he had tried to steal a pup from an earlier litter last year. When Talon started to take flight with the a pup in the previous attempt, Thunder had made a tremendous leap and sank his teeth into one of

Talon's legs, causing the eagle to drop the pup. But Thunder lost his grip on Talon and fell back to the ground. Talon managed to escape with his life by only the narrowest of margins. As Talon flew off, he shrieked at Thunder, "There will be another day when you won't be so lucky!"

Thunder growled in reply, "If you come back here and threaten my family, I will kill you!" That pup was Raul. Raul survived, but his body still bore the scars from Talon's claws.

Aiyana haltingly barked, "The eagle said…to tell Thunder… thanks for the meal."

Thunder growled at the now empty sky. "Talon, I promised I would kill you if you came back. I will keep that promise."

By then Shadow and the rest of the pack had arrived. Upon learning of Talon's raid and the loss of Zev, all the wolves began a chorus of mournful howls that originated from the very depths of their being. The surviving pups began to emerge from the den. Shadow and the rest of the wolves gave special attention to each pup, licking and nuzzling them. Blood Warrior liked the affection but only to a certain point. He kept looking at the vacant sky and growling. Blood Warrior didn't want or need to be comforted. What he really wanted was to sink his teeth into the eagle who had killed his brother.

Even is the midst of her own sorrow, Shadow licked and comforted Aiyana. "It was not your fault, my sweet daughter. There was nothing you could do." The rest of the pack gathered around Aiyana, giving her consoling and comforting licks and nuzzles.

Aiyana would never forget the horrors of that day. While everyone in the pack would also remember, only two of the wolves swore revenge in the hearts. Of course, Thunder was one, but the rest of the wolves would have been surprised to know that the other was the young pup, Blood Warrior.

After viciously crushing Zev with his claws as he flew, Talon carried the now lifeless pup's body to his nest at the top of a 200-foot Douglas fir tree. At least Zev was spared the agony of being eaten alive. Talon ripped the pup's body apart as he devoured Zev. Zev's skull and bones littered the eagle's nest along with many others, but the rest of Zev's remains could only be found in the scat of Talon.

A flock of crows made derisive caws at Talon as they winged by the nest. Of course they maintained a safe distance. Despite their raucous bravado, they wanted nothing to do with the great eagle.

DARK DEMON

T he roar of the monstrous silvertip grizzly bear caused all the animals within hearing range to freeze. Demon loved that all the animals were terrified of him. His fur was a deep chocolate brown with the tips of each hair colored white. Demon stood six feet tall at the shoulder when he was on all fours. When he stood on his hind legs, he stretched out to over twelve feet. Demon weighed over 2,000 pounds, which dwarfed most adult grizzlies who average 1,500 pounds.

While Demon had the same concerns and desires of most grizzlies, he had a special passion for killing wolves. Devouring wolves put him into an orgasmic state of frenzy.

Demon's desire to kill wolves was fueled by the memory of a pack of wolves who had killed one of his litter-mates as he watched when he was a cub. The attack on the grizzly mother and her two cubs was unusual for wolves. It had been a hard winter and the wolves were driven by acute hunger. There were just too many wolves for the mother grizzly to protect both cubs. She was able to save Demon but not her other cub.

Demon would eat anything, plants as well as meat. At one time or another, he had dined on moose, elk, caribou, deer, bighorn sheep, mountain goats and black bears. Demon was also not above cannibalism as he would readily kill and eat other grizzlies. He was a deadly combination of a glutton and a killing machine, both of which accounted for his huge size.

Despite their size difference, Barky enjoyed harassing Demon. "Hey lard ass, you might mix in a few more plants once in a while! If someone told you to haul your big ass out of here, you'd have to make four trips!"

Demon looked at Barky as the squirrel jumped from tree to tree and roared with exasperation, "If I ever get my paws on you, I will eat your scrawny body in a hundred tiny bites! I will pay you back for your insults!"

Barky laughed. "I'm not the least bit worried about a dumb shit like you catching me."

Demon scented the wolves before they smelled him. Ulrich and Aiyana were upwind from Demon as they were stalking a young moose who was munching on Elk Sedge. Even with his incredible bulk, Demon could move silently and swiftly through the forest. With a savage roar, Demon was on Aiyana before she could react. He broke her back with one swipe of his huge paw. She thrashed and whined pitifully, "Ulrich, I'm hurt! Help me! Please save me!" Aiyana tried to get up but her legs were no longer working.

Ulrich courageously but foolishly tried to come to his sister's rescue as he growled, "I'm coming Aiyana!"

Ulrich knew his only chance was to blind the big bear. He charged in and jumped at Demon's eyes, viciously snapping his teeth. Unfortunately, his bite was just an inch short of his target. The suddenness of Ulrich's attack and the near success of almost blinding him caused Demon to jerk backward, losing his balance and falling over. Demon lumbered to his feet and began swinging his head back and forth as he bared his huge teeth.

Demon snarled, "Nice try wolf, but not good enough. You cannot defeat me! It's ridiculous that you even tried. You are going to die right here and right now!"

Ulrich growled back, "Don't be so sure, bear! I am a son of Thunder, the greatest wolf fighter of all time!"

Demon gave a low chuckle. "That's some dumb shit, wolf. Ten wolves could not defeat me, much less just one."

Ulrich leaped again at his eyes, but Demon grabbed Ulrich in mid-flight with his giant jaws and snapped Ulrich's body in two. Looking down on the two wolves, Demon grunted, "You're not the brightest wolves I've ever seen. But, at least you will serve a useful purpose by providing me something good to eat." Ulrich was already dead. Aiyana died when Demon ripped her entire stomach out with one bite.

Demon feasted on their bodies, snapping his jaws together and roaring with delight. His beady, pig-like eyes twinkled with joy. Killing and eating wolves made this a great day for him. All the other animals within the sound of Demon's roar slipped away as quietly and as quickly as they could. Even the birds in the surrounding trees flew away, nervously squawking and chirping. None wanted to be within miles of the giant grizzly.

When Ulrich and Aiyana did not return to the pack that night, Thunder went looking for them at daylight the next morning. Shadow wanted to go with him but Thunder told her, "I need you to stay here and help protect the others."

The sky had clouded up and a soft rain was falling. A thunderhead promised a harder rain would be coming. There was a light ground fog, giving daybreak an eerie feeling. Thunder picked up the faint foot scent of Ulrich and Aiyana and began to track them. A foreboding came over him when he began to smell the rank odor of Demon.

Thunder found the spot where his children had been killed and eaten. There were bits and pieces of their hides and a few splintered bones. Thunder knew they were the remains of Ulrich and Aiyana. The scent of the giant grizzly was still strong, telling Thunder that the bear was close by. Thunder was no coward, but he also knew he was no match for Demon. He quietly left what was now the gravesite of two of his children and dejectedly returned to the den.

When Shadow saw the hard look on Thunder's face, she howled, "Dear Father Wolf, no! I can't take any more losses of my children!" For three days, Shadow was inconsolable and would not eat. Finally, Thunder brought her favorite meal, a fresh deer kill. Thunder licked and nuzzled her. "Shadow, I know you are hurting for our dead children. I hurt for them too but we have living children who are depending on us. You will sicken and die if you don't eat. I can take just about anything but I couldn't take losing you. Please, for the sake of your living family, eat."

Only then did Shadow begin to feed. The life-giving meat and blood not only revived her body, it also revived her spirit.

The rest of the wolves in the pack howled for days in grief and sadness at the deaths of Ulrich and Aiyana. The weather was rainy and dreary. It seemed the very heavens were also mourning.

Six months passed and the remaining four pups grew strong and healthy, but none came close to matching the size of Blood Warrior, who now weighed over 100 pounds. He was already one of the best hunters in the pack, second only to Thunder.

GLUTTON

Wolverines are considered one of the toughest predators pound for pound in the animal kingdom, none more so than Glutton. While Demon was a glutton in his own right, he was no match for the stocky, muscular wolverine in the appetite department. Glutton's ferocity and strength were out of proportion to the size of his body, enabling him to kill animals much larger than himself.

He had dark brown fur with lighter stripes of brown down each side of his body. The same light brown color created a mask on his face. He was the size of a large dog, weighing in at a little over 60 pounds. Glutton's broad head, short stubby ears, and small, round eyes gleaming with malice, and coupled with the strength of his jaws it caused even the largest of predators to be reluctant to attack him.

Instead of marking his territory with urine, Glutton marked it with a rank-smelling scent gland that caused some animals to refer to him as "skunk bear."

Glutton loved to eat. Constantly. He would eat anything from a mouse to a moose, alive or rotting carrion made no difference to him. Glutton once attacked and killed a small grizzly bear by latching onto its throat and stubbornly hanging on until it suffocated to death. He viewed everything as a potential meal.

When Barky saw Glutton, he said, "Well, looky here. It's the only son of a bitch in the entire forest who's fatter and uglier than that big stupid grizzly bear, Demon. Hey Glutton, I think I know why your parents never taught you anything. How old were you when you ate them? Why don't I ever see any of your wolverine offspring? Is it because you ate your mate? Did you eat her right away or did you wait until she was pregnant so she would be a little fatter? That is, if you even have a mate! Come to think of it, what type of nitwit would breed with you? You would probably have to poke her eyes out first if she didn't beat you to it and poke out her own eyes!"

Glutton bared his sharp teeth, "Barky, you are not the first to underestimate me. That has proven to be a fatal mistake to others!"

Barky smirked, "How in the hell is it possible to underestimate you? Underestimate a slug? That's possible. Underestimate a beetle? That's possible. Underestimate you? That would be impossible!"

The pack had gone several days without a kill. Their stomachs were rumbling with hunger. Thunder barked, "Everyone hunts today except for Shadow. Shadow, I need you to stay and keep the pups safe." Shadow didn't argue as lately she wouldn't let the pups out of her sight. She wanted to stay and be with them.

Thunder said to Blood Warrior, "Son, you come with me." This was not the first time Thunder had chosen Blood Warrior as his hunting partner. The first time he chose Blood Warrior, all the wolves were a little surprised that he had selected someone so young, but now everyone was used to Blood Warrior hunting with his father.

The wolves scattered in different directions to find game. The day was overcast with just a faint breeze, which all in all made for good scenting conditions and a great day for hunting.

Larentia and Landga were hunting together when they spotted Glutton. Larentia said with a low growl, "We are bigger and outnumber him. Besides, I am hungry. Let's kill and eat this skunk bear." Glutton saw them coming but made no attempt to hide or run. The only animal in the forest that Glutton feared enough to run from was the massive Demon. When the female wolves approached him, circling and wary, Glutton smugly thought to himself, *No one dares attack the great Glutton.*

Larentia growled a threat, "Skunk bear, you're looking good today. Do you taste as good as you look?" Langda snickered at Larentia's remark.

Glutton bared his sharp teeth, "You two idiots will never find that out but I may find out how good you taste. I'm surprised that Thunder didn't warn you about me."

Larentia barked, "Our father did warn us but sometimes he is too cautious. My sister and I can handle the likes of you." The sisters had worked as a team on many kills. All wolves preferred causing their prey to run, as this exposed their vital areas more readily. Sometimes they killed immediately, but if their prey was larger, they might have to run it to ground to wear it down before slaying it.

A bluejay, perched on a limb, squawked a warning to the wolves. Neither wolf paid any attention to the irritating bird.

The wolves made several feints trying to get Glutton to move one way or the other. But he just arched his back and bristled his fur. His fur standing on end made him look much larger than he actually was. Finally Langda said, "Father forgot to tell us that you were such a coward, Glutton! I am just a girl, one of the weakest in our pack. Yet you are terrified of me. Are you sure that you're not a female wolverine? Spread your legs and let's see if you even have anything dangling there. I think you might be hiding a birth canal!"

As the sisters continued to circle, Larentia chimed in, "How many litters have you had, Glutton? Maybe you have not given birth after all because what self-respecting wolverine would have the stomach to mate with you?" Langda hooted with laughter.

When Langda laughed, her head came up slightly, causing her to lose sight of Glutton for a fraction of a second. That was enough of an opening for the lightening quick wolverine to lock his powerful jaws around her throat and shake her violently. Her neck snapped and Langda whimpered a couple of times before her legs gave a dying flutter. From start to finish, it took Langda less than five seconds to die.

For the next few moments, Larentia was frozen in shock from the sight of the killing of her treasured sister. She suddenly awoke from her trance, bared her teeth with a snarl and charged Glutton. She was furious over the death of Langda. Her initial charge knocked down the wolverine, but he quickly sprang back to his feet in a defensive posture. Larentia growled, "You are going to pay with your blood for killing my sister!"

They came together, biting and clawing each other. Larentia had the upper hand on Glutton as she was bending the wolverine backward. Glutton suddenly gave way to the pressure, causing Larentia to lose her balance. Glutton rolled under her, knocking her down. He grabbed her throat with his deadly jaws as she lay on her back. She could not make a sound as Glutton choked her down. What Larentia could not vocalize, she communicated in her horror-stricken eyes. Just as she was about to die from lack of oxygen, Glutton loosened his death grip on her throat.

Glutton felt he had been cheated in the first wolf's death. It was too fast. He had been robbed of the full joy of the kill. This time as Larentia lay fighting for breath, alive but near death, Glutton gloated, "Why am I not hearing all the smart-ass remarks from you two wolf bitches? What's wrong? Wolverine got your tongue?" Glutton laughed hysterically at his own joke.

Glutton spoke to the dead Langda and the almost-dead Larentia. "You were very concerned about my sex. If you could see, you would see that I'm a fully developed male. But maybe you should have been more worried about my teeth." The wolverine began to eat. Blood and slobber drooled from his lethal jaws. Glutton winked at the now-dead corpses, "I have to say that today has been glorious. I can't remember when I've enjoyed killing and eating wolves any more than I have today."

Larentia's last thought before succumbing to death was, *I wish I had listened to Father.*

When Langda and Larentia did not return from the hunt that night, Thunder and Shadow exchanged looks of dread. Shadow began to sadly howl, "Father Wolf, do not kill any more of my children! Please, kill me instead!"

Thunder nudged Shadow hard to get her attention. "Shadow, you know that Father Wolf has not killed our children. They were a gift from Him. Why would he kill them? The ones who have died were not killed by His hand."

At dawn, Thunder started the search for their two daughters. It was a bright, sunny, late autumn day with several hummingbirds helicoptering in the air. Even the sight of the hummingbirds did not cheer up Thunder's heavy heart. By sniffing the air and the ground, Thunder was able to trail Langda and Larentia. Within a few hours, Thunder found what was left of them. The smell of Glutton was overpowering. He could see the tracks of the wolves where they had circled the wolverine. Glutton had left precious little of Langda and Larentia, just a little hide and considerable blood stains on the earth and leaves. Thunder could see where Glutton had actually licked the ground, not wanting to waste any of their blood. His first instinct was to follow Glutton and kill him, but he knew that Shadow was anxiously awaiting his return.

There was a weariness in the eyes of Thunder as he approached Shadow. Shadow didn't even howl. She just dropped to the ground, her body shaking with sobs. Thunder tried to console her but she was lost in her grief. Thunder thought, *When will this nightmare end? I don't know what else to say to Shadow.* This time it took Shadow several weeks to lessen her mourning and focus on her living family again.

SLY COUGAR

Sly was a sleek, fully-mature cougar. She was ill-tempered, even for a mountain lion. Cougars are notorious for being hard to get along with, including their own kind. Sly had killed her last mate in a dispute over the split of a moose kill. Her mate, Leo, had complained, "Why is it that you always get to divide our kills? And, why is it you always get the biggest portions?" Sly responded by savagely slicing Leo up with her teeth and claws. Sly ate her portion of the moose, Leo's portion of the moose and polished it off by eating Leo. She never felt better.

Even though she was a female, Sly was the largest mountain lion in the territory, weighing almost 300 pounds. There were very few animals, including bigger predators, who didn't tense up when they heard Sly scream in the dead of night. During the day, her tawny coat shined a golden hue when the sun caught it just right. Sly's powerful hind legs could catapult her up to a limb that was 20 feet off the group in one bound. She could safely clear a 50-foot gorge with a thrust of her powerful hind legs. Sly was capable of short bursts of speed of 50 mph. She was a formidable and dangerous killer.

Sly crouched on an aspen limb high off the ground, her long tail hanging down and slowly twitching back and forth. She watched Raul slowly stalk a yearling elk. Sly carefully stood up on the limb and stretched herself. She was interested in two things. One, stealing Raul's kill if he had a successful hunt, and two, killing and eating Raul himself.

Sly was sick to death of hearing other animals talk about what a great hunter Thunder was. She knew she was a much better hunter but no one gave her any credit. Others were too busy bragging on Thunder. Sly thought to herself, *I hate that damn Thunder. If I could kill one of his sons, it would be perfect. I could fill my stomach and cause pain to Thunder all at the same time.*

Raul had a death grip on the young elk's throat, already savoring the delicious taste of its flesh. He never smelled nor saw Sly. Raul and the elk were bowled over by Sly's charge. Both the hunter and the hunted sprang back to their feet. Sly began to slowly circle the startled Raul. Raul bowed up and growled as he bluffed, "Cat, you better get your stupid ass up a tree if you know what's good for you!"

Sly laughed, "You are either very brave or very dumb! In the end, it doesn't really make much of a difference. You will be dead either way."

Despite his threats, Raul knew he was facing certain death if he didn't do something. He briefly considered running but discarded that idea when he realized he could not outrun her. Raul's best chance was to attack. He took two steps to his left and then cut back to his right trying to get Sly leaning one way and exposing her belly. Raul got his teeth in her side but Sly slapped him away with one of her big paws.

Sly took the offensive. Nothing fancy, just a straight power move. She simply ran over him, sending him flying. Sly immediately pounced on him, clamping down on Raul's throat, blocking the vital oxygen needed to sustain life. In the meantime, the young elk was able to stagger away without the wolf's jaws strangling her. As the life ebbed from Raul, Sly casually noted the direction the injured elk took. Sly would eventually track the elk and finish the job and the meal that Raul started.

When Sly started to feed on Raul's body, she screamed, "Thunder, I have killed one of your foul offspring! I am thankful you are a good breeder! I can always use an easy meal!" The forlorn cry of a yellow billed loon from a nearby lake completed the melancholy mood of the death of Raul.

When Raul didn't return to the pack that night, Thunder and Shadow gave each other a desolate look of having seen this awful story before. Shadow whimpered, "I can't take much more of this. If something has happened to Raul..."

Thunder barked, "Don't jump to conclusions. I will go look for him." Thunder tried to hide his true feelings but there was a knot in the pit of his stomach that told him the outcome was not going to be good.

Thunder tracked Raul to a sumac thicket where he found Raul's remains. When Thunder analyzed the kill site and saw Sly's tracks and smelled her scent, he thought, *I just thought I hated Sly before. I will not rest until I see her dead.* As much as he mourned the death of his son, Thunder dreaded even more having to tell the terrible news to Shadow.

When Shadow saw the downcast look on Thunder's face, she threw back her head and made a piercing, keening howl, "Father Wolf, what have I done for you to punish me so? Whatever it is, I'm sorry! I'm sorry!"

The pack was now reduced down to Thunder, Shadow and this year's pups: Digger, Nashoba, Otsandra and Blood Warrior. All the wolves joined in the sorrowful howling. One wolf's howls were a little different. One wolf's howls carried threats of retribution. One wolf's howls promised revenge. That wolf was not Thunder. It was the young Blood Warrior.

RED FANG

W olf packs use urine to mark their territories. The markings tell strange wolves to stay away. It was not unusual for an interloper to be killed by a pack protecting their territory. One pack leader who systematically and methodically destroyed any stray wolf unlucky enough or stupid enough to blunder into his territory was Red Fang.

While wolves are a feared predator, they usually kill just for food. Red Fang was an exception. He was a particularly cruel and merciless wolf who sometimes killed just for the joy of killing. He was the alpha male for his lawless pack. Red Fang did not respect the laws handed down from Father Wolf. He allowed his offspring to stay with the pack and interbreed with each other. His pack numbered 19 wolves, three or four times the size of a regular pack. Red Fang's mate was Delilah, but Red Fang didn't restrict his mating to just her. He would also breed his own daughters and granddaughters. Thus, most of his inbred children were mental morons. Red Fang actually preferred that. He didn't want his pack members to think—just obey.

To maintain his authority in the pack, Red Fang would viciously bite any pack member regardless of age or sex. With hunger being his only provocation, he had also killed and eaten several of his own offspring, including a few new-born pups. The wolves in his pack witnessed his callous murdering and devouring of their brothers and sisters. It was a well-noted testament of the pack leader's indifference to his children and grandchildren. They knew if they did not immediately obey his commands, the best thing that could happen was a painful bite. The worst thing would be a trip down his throat, through his stomach and intestines, and out his anus.

Two of Red Fang's sons, Adolph and Brutus, were next in command of their pack. Adolph and Brutus were just as ruthless as their father. They each harbored dreams of killing their father and taking over the leadership of the pack. Each tried to keep his ambitions hidden from Red Fang as well as from each other. The cunning Red Fang knew what was in their hearts. He never let his guard down with them. He even used their ambitions against each other. Red Fang was able to coax more effort out of each by bragging to one about how well the other one was doing.

Even Red Fang was not exempt from Barky's barbs. "Hey Red Fang, are all your kids idiots? Dear Father Squirrel, do they have to drool all over everything? You would think the law of averages would get you at least one that would be smarter than a pine cone!"

Red Fang growled menacingly, "One day, Barky, you will fall. When you do, I will be there to catch you."

Barky responded, "I doubt that will ever happen but if it does, tell those imbeciles you call children that I said to kiss my ass. Of course, you'll have to show them which end is the ass!"

The first time Thunder and Red Fang met, neither had their packs with them although Thunder was accompanied by Shadow and Red Fang was with Adolph and Brutus. As they cautiously circled each other, Red Fang bared his teeth and snarled, "Soooo, you must be the great Thunder I've heard so much about. Are all of the things that they say about you true?"

Thunder responded, "It depends on what you've heard. You must be Red Fang. Surely, all the things I've heard about you can't be true. No wolf can be that big an asshole."

Red Fang bristled and growled, "Watch your mouth, Thunder. I would hate to make the lovely Shadow a widow." Red Fang then gave Shadow a suggestive leer.

Thunder raised his tail and arched his back in a show of dominance. "You are on dangerous ground, Red Fang! If I choose to kill you, you will die and your two simpletons will not be able to save you."

Red Fang glanced at Adolph and Brutus and briefly considered attacking Thunder and Shadow but decided to wait until the odds were more heavily in his favor. Red Fang snarled, "I am feeling generous today, Thunder. I'm going to let you live. Tomorrow you may not be so fortunate!"

Thunder sneered, "I am not surprised that you would turn tail and run. It's what I would expect from a wolf that is so disrespectful to Father Wolf. You are a disgrace to all true wolves. I pray that Father Wolf will use me one day to bring your miserable life to an end."

Red Fang and his two sons slunk back into the cover of the brushy sumac with its fern-like leaves and red berries. After they had disappeared, Thunder was still angry and growling. Shadow tried to calm him, "It's all right now, Thunder. They're gone."

Thunder barked, "After finally meeting him, I really hate Red Fang. I can't stand the sight of him!" It took another hour for the fur on his neck to settle back down to its natural state of ease.

One day, Brutus came running up to Red Fang and breathlessly barked, "Father, I have spied on Thunder's pack as you commanded. Thunder and his big pup have left Shadow with the other pups while they go hunting." Red Fang ordered six of the adult wolves, including Brutus and Adolph, to follow him as he loped to where Brutus had last seen Shadow and her pups.

Shadow, Digger, Nashoba and Otsandra were resting as they leisurely napped in the shade of a stand of pines. A sharp noise in the fallen leaves made all four wolves jump to attention. Shadow could not see anything. Then she heard the laughing chatter of a squirrel who had just thrown a nut to try to scare them. Seeing Barky, Shadow said, "Barky! I am going to spank you with my tail if you don't behave yourself!"

Barky continued to snicker, "I'm just trying to help you stay alert, Shadow. Don't you want me to keep you on your toes?"

Shadow responded, "Keep it up and you're not going to have any toes!"

The wolves laid back down and were starting to doze again when Shadow heard another noise in the leaves, "Barky, you are going to get it!" But this time it wasn't Barky.

Shadow blanched and stepped back when the sinister Red Fang stepped out from behind a tree. Shadow barked, "Children, get behind me, now!" The half-grown pups dutifully took their places behind their mother. Shadow demanded of Red Fang, "What are you doing here? Thunder will be back any minute. He will kill you if he finds you here! You better go—now!"

Red Fang just laughed, "I know that the great Thunder and his coyote of a son are a long way from here. You and the rest of his disgusting spawn are all alone."

Shadow sputtered, "What do you want?"

Red Fang growled, "I am going to kill all of you but I will give you a chance to live. I will not kill you if you agree to join my pack and be my mate."

Shadow knew that this was now a matter of life and death. She shakily said, "I will go with you if you will let my pups live." Shadow thought, *Even if I have to go with him, Thunder will come save me.* To their credit Digger, Nashoba and Otsandra were not cowed down, but were growling warnings at the strange wolves.

Red Fang approached Shadow until his ugly nose was mere inches from hers, "No one dictates terms to me. I say who lives and who dies! Your children are already as good as dead! But you can live. Choose!"

Shadow protested, "No. I can... not..." Red Fang cut her off with a command to his pack, "Kill them!"

As Red Fang stepped away to watch the slaughter, his six wolves attacked Shadow and the pups. Shadow seemed like she was every place at once. Otsandra had been knocked down and was on her back being savaged by sharp teeth and claws. Shadow leapt to her defense, biting down hard on the attacker's neck. The wolf yipped as Shadow felt the crunch of his neck bone as it broke into two pieces.

Digger and Nashoba were back to back and surprisingly holding their own against the larger wolves' assault as they fought tooth and nail. Digger shocked Red Fang and his followers as he tore out the throat of one of the attacking wolves. This caused the four remaining henchmen to temporarily halt their blitz in astonishment.

Shadow took advantage of the pause, shouting, "Quick children, follow me!" Despite the blood flowing from their wounds, Shadow and the pups sprinted away. Red Fang snarled at the top of his lungs, "After them, you idiots! You're letting them get away!"

Otsandra was the most injured and the slowest of the four as she ran with a limp. Shadow could see that the pursuing wolves were gaining and would catch them. She slid to a stop and quickly barked, "Children, remember how quail sleep at night?" The pups knew that quail formed a circle with the tails pointed in and their heads pointed out. The pups nodded and quickly formed a defensive circle with their tails touching.

Red Fang and his marauders surveyed the ring of flashing teeth. Red Fang spewed more of his venom as he addressed his pack members, "It's a sad day in wolfdom when members of my pack are defeated by one bitch and three pups! I am ashamed to call you my kin! Now, finish them or I will finish you!"

The renegades attacked with a renewed fervor as they knew if they didn't succeed, Red Fang would kill them. Otsandra was the first to go down. Shadow and Digger turned to try to defend her, even though it meant exposing themselves to their own attackers. Shadow and Digger fought savagely but they were trying to save Otsandra while also defending themselves.

Otsandra, who had dreamed of being like Shadow and being the matriarch of her own pack, died from an extreme loss of blood without seeing those dreams realized. Her death freed up her killer to join the others in their onslaught. Nashoba's vision started to blur. She would have given anything to have seen a beautiful butterfly one more time. The light of life went out in her eyes as her neck snapped from the bite from one of the renegades.

Shadow's and Digger's fighting spirits were renewed as they now fought not only for their own lives but for revenge for the deaths of Otsandra and Nashoba. The two of them fought their four opponents to a stalemate. Disgusted, Red

Fang snorted, "Wolf shit! Do I have to do everything myself?" as he joined the fight.

Belatedly, Shadow tried to signal Thunder with a howl but Red Fang clamped his jaws around her throat before she could make a sound. He shook the weakened Shadow. Her eyes darted from side to side hoping to see Thunder, but she died in the jaws of Red Fang. The four other renegades soon killed Digger. He did not stand a chance against such overwhelming numbers but he never quit. He fought until his last breath.

Red Fang stopped his pack from feeding, "No! No one eats them! I want you to tear them into little pieces!" Red Fang wanted as shocking a scene as possible for Thunder. He wanted the fear and respect that Thunder had not shown him when they first met.

Red Fang's demented monsters ripped off the legs from the bodies. Then, the paws from the legs. Their heads were chewed from the bodies. Their bodies wound up dissected into small pieces. Once Red Fang was satisfied with the carnage, he led his group of murderers back to the safety of the big pack. Red Fang said to Adolph and Brutus, "Too bad the stupid bitch made the wrong decision. I would have shared her with the two of you. But at least, we put that big-shot Thunder in his place."

What Red Fang did not know was just before he showed himself to Shadow, he and his marauders were spotted by Barky. For once the jokester was serious. Barky recognized that death was imminent for Shadow and the pups. He fully extended the thin membranes of skin on each side of his body that gave him his "wings" and, unseen by Red Fang, began gliding from tree to tree, frantically searching for Thunder.

Barky found Thunder and Blood Warrior in the final stage of a stalk on a deer. Barky breathlessly shouted, "Thunder!" The deer bolted at the sound of the bark from the squirrel.

Thunder, exasperated, growled, "Barky, that's not funny!"

As he got his breath back, Barky shouted, "It's Shadow and the pups! Red Fang is there! Come quick!"

Thunder and Blood Warrior ran the entire way back to the den. They skidded to a stop as they couldn't believe the horror of the scene at the den. The heads and the small pieces of the bodies of Shadow, Digger, Nashoba and Otsandra were almost too much to comprehend. The whole area was painted in blood.

Thunder's howl was filled with rage. "Damn you, Red Fang! I will kill you and your entire pack of misfits!"

Blood Warrior was bristling and growling in agreement. "Yes Father, we will kill them all!" Even in the midst of the most intense grief that he had ever experienced, Thunder stopped and thought about his last surviving offspring and his future.

Finally, he spoke to Blood Warrior, "You cannot come with me. I must go but I have something even more important for you to do."

Blood Warrior was bewildered. "Father, what could possibly be more important than our revenge on Red Fang?"

Thunder replied, "This will be hard for you, but I want you to wait here for the outcome of my attack on Red Fang and his pack. There is a chance that I won't come back. If I am killed, I want you to leave this territory, find a mate and start your own pack."

Blood Warrior protested, "But Father, together we could wipe them out!"

Thunder responded, "Your survival and the continuation of our family is more important to me. I want your promise that you will honor my command."

Blood Warrior continued to argue, but Thunder stood firm. Finally, Blood Warrior submitted. "Father, I will do as you command me. But how will I know what happens to you?"

Thunder said, "When Barky gets back, ask him to follow me and report back to you."

Blood Warrior nuzzled Thunder and softly barked, "Be careful Father. Come back to me."

Thunder loped off but stopped before he got out of sight. "Blood Warrior, remember your promise to me!" Blood Warrior reluctantly nodded his head in acknowledgement.

BATTLE OF THUNDER

I n a few minutes, Barky glided in to a nearby tree. The little squirrel was shocked at the massacre. "Father Squirrel! All in the animal kingdom understand killing for food. It is our world. But, this… this… this is madness!" Barky then looked at Blood Warrior. "Young wolf, I am so sorry. Is there anything I can do to help?"

Blood Warrior said, "My father has gone after Red Fang. Please follow him and tell me what happens."

Barky replied, "I'm on my way!" as he glided off in pursuit of Thunder.

Content that he had provided a plan and a future for Blood Warrior, Thunder allowed the white-hot anger of revenge to take over and consume him. Thunder thought of all the animals who had killed each of the other members of his pack. He was ashamed that he had promised revenge for each death but had not fulfilled any of his promises. Thunder vowed to himself, *I have not brought to justice any of those who I had sworn to hold accountable. But this time, I will sacrifice everything including my own life to avenge Shadow and my children.* He knew that he stood very little chance against that many wolves, but the atrocities that had been done to Shadow and the pups put him into a killing rage. Thunder vowed to kill as many of them as he could, especially Red Fang.

Thunder made no attempt at stealth or concealment. Red Fang had set out sentinels to warn him of Thunder's approach. Red Fang knew Thunder would come. He wanted him to come. As soon as Red Fang heard the warning howl of one of the sentinels, he lined up his best fighters to be between him and the charge of Thunder.

Night had fallen but a large silver moon had risen. The light from the moon and stars illuminated the forest. Thunder's vision was as clear as if it had been daylight.

When Thunder broke into the clearing where the pack was waiting, he was already traveling at a high rate of speed. He not only didn't check his speed at the sight of the overwhelming numbers but he shifted into his fastest sprint as he growled and bared his teeth. Thunder had no fear, but most of the other wolves did not have any fear either. Thunder's lack of fear was due to his courage. Red Fang's wolves' lack of fear was due to the fact they were functioning idiots.

Thunder hit the first row of wolves, knocking most of them off their feet. He was able to tear the throat out of one before being swarmed. Thunder shouted as he desperately fought, "I am going to kill you, Red Fang!" He killed one more before their many bites began to take effect on his body.

Red Fang taunted, "Well, come on, Thunder! I'm standing right here!" Red Fang's courage was bolstered by the knowledge that Thunder could not get through his pack to bite him.

As Thunder lay dying, Adolph and Brutus rushed in to finish him off, fighting each other for the bragging rights of being known as the wolf who killed Thunder. When Thunder's body was limp and lifeless, Red Fang and his pack howled in victory.

Barky could not stand it anymore and made his presence known from the top of a tall pine tree. "Red Fang, you and your gang of freaks are going to get what's coming to you one day! It may not be today or even tomorrow, but one day, it will happen!"

Red Fang smirked, "Squirrel, you are a nobody. You are nothing! What you say is just a small breeze blowing through the trees."

Barky then watched in horror as Red Fang commanded his wolves to tear Thunder's body into little pieces as he had them do to Shadow. Reluctantly, Barky glided back to where Blood Warrior was waiting for him. As Blood Warrior looked up with a hopeful expression, Barky dashed his hopes. "Blood Warrior, you should be proud of your father. I have never seen anyone fight as bravely and as fiercely as Thunder!"

Blood Warrior gave a mournful, sad howl as he stood among the pitiful remains of his once proud family. A great horned owl sat on a high limb in stunned silence at the massacre of the wolves. Blood Warrior made a vow to himself that he would avenge the killings of his family members. Every night he would recite his death list of murderers to himself: *Demon, Glutton, Talon, Sly, Red Fang and his entire pack.* Blood Warrior would never forget.

Blood Warrior said to Barky, "I made a promise to my father and I'm going to keep it. I am leaving this territory to find a mate to begin my own pack. That will fulfill my commitment to Thunder. But once that has been done, I'm coming back to take my revenge!"

As Blood Warrior loped off, Barky called after him, "I hope you're blessed by Father Squirrel, my friend! I will watch for your return!" Blood Warrior did not look back but flicked his ears to acknowledge that he heard Barky. He set his face to the rising moon, determined that he would succeed where his beloved father had failed.

TASHA

———————

T he season turned to winter. Winter in the North
Country usually lasts five months. This winter was
unusually harsh, with a number of freezing snow and
ice storms. In spite of the conditions, Blood Warrior was a
successful hunter and was able kill enough game to store fat
on his body. He now weighed over 300 pounds, which was
twice the size of the normal male timber wolf. He occasionally
heard and responded to other wolf howls. Blood Warrior
approached other packs but they all warned him away with
unwelcoming growls. He could have easily killed the alpha
males and taken over any of the packs but he just couldn't
bring himself to kill another wolf who was just trying to
protect his family. Blood Warrior did not want another wolf
family to endure the pain and agony that his own family had
suffered.

Spring brought the big thaw. The woods and pastures were
adorned with the brilliant colors of wildflowers; purple mon-
keyflowers, orange Indian paintbrushes and yellow showy
goldeneyes. Blood Warrior heard the honking of Canadian
geese and trumpeter swans as they returned from the south
to their breeding grounds.

One night under a full moon, Blood Warrior heard a wolf howl that snapped his head around. There was something about this howl. It was different from any wolf howl he had ever heard. Blood Warrior immediately answered with his own howl. When his howl was returned, Blood Warrior trotted in the direction of the howling of the strange wolf.

As he neared the source of the howling, Blood Warrior smelled the sweet scent of the twinberry honeysuckle. He skirted a sumac thicket and came into an opening in the forest. Under the light of the full moon, Blood Warrior saw the most beautiful wolf that he had ever seen. She was sleek with lustrous blond fur.

If Blood Warrior was the ultimate in wolf masculinity, this female was his equal in wolf femininity. Blood Warrior approached her cautiously as he didn't want to scare her off. He gently nuzzled her neck and licked her jaw. Blood Warrior was stunned as he looked into the brightest, bluest eyes that he had ever seen. He softly barked, "I am Blood Warrior. What is your name?"

She shyly responded, "I am called Tasha."

Blood Warrior replied, "You are beautiful!" Tasha was completely taken with him, admiring his thick black fur and glistening golden eyes.

Tasha returned Blood Warrior's licks. She was already in season and was ready to breed. As is the wolf's custom, Blood Warrior wasted no time as he mounted her from behind. Tasha moved her tail to the side to allow Blood Warrior access to her body. After the coupling was completed, the two wolves spent the rest of the night mating repeatedly, licking and nuzzling each other. At the end of the first night, both wolves knew that they had found their mate for life. The entire night Blood Warrior smelled the aroma of the sweet honeysuckle. For the rest of his life, the scent from honeysuckle always reminded him of their first night together.

Blood Warrior and Tasha told each other the story of their lives. Tasha was horrified at the story of his family, "Oh, Dear Father Wolf! Honey, I am so sorry! You are so strong to survive all those horrible tragedies!" Tasha's background was more typical of the average wolf. Her father and mother had taught her to hunt and survive on her own. When she became ready to breed, she left her pack to find her own mate. Tasha had been sad to leave her family but was excited to begin her adult life.

DOLT

While Tasha could not match Blood Warrior's strength—no wolf could— she made up for it in speed and cunning. Together they made a formidable hunting team. One day while hunting, Tasha cocked her ears and barked, "Wait, what was that?"

Blood Warrior responded, "What? I don't hear anything."

Tasha said, "Shush, listen." In a minute they both heard a soft whimpering noise. They saw a slight movement in the leaves of the sumac.

Blood Warrior bristled as he growled, "Whatever you are, come out and show yourself!" There was no response. Blood Warrior demanded, "Come out now! If you don't come out and I have to come in after you, I will kill you!" After a few more moments, the limbs parted and a gray wolf slunk out of the brush. He immediately turned on his back in total submission as he peed on himself. Blood Warrior was astonished at the skinny, emaciated body. The wolf probably only weighed 50 pounds. Blood Warrior thought, *This is the poorest excuse for a wolf that I've ever seen.*

Tasha barked softly to the strange wolf, "You poor thing. What is your name?"

There was another pause and the wolf whined, "My father named me Dolt."

At that point Blood Warrior, who was already disgusted at the sight of the wolf, growled, "Why would a father name his own pup Dolt?"

Dolt stammered, "He... he...sa-said that I wa-was worthless and a coward."

Blood Warrior retorted, "Why would your father call you a coward?"

Dolt closed his eyes for a minute and lay still. Finally, he lifted his head and said, "It's because I'm pretty much afraid of everything."

Blood Warrior was puzzled,. "What kinds of things are you afraid of?"

Dolt answered, "Well, to begin with, deer scare the crap out of me."

Blood Warrior burst out laughing as he thought Dolt was joking. When he saw that Dolt wasn't joking, he barked loudly, "What kind of wolf is afraid of deer? Wolves *EAT* deer!"

Tasha interrupted, "Hush! Can't you see he's scared? We should help him, not scare him!"

Dolt tried to explain, "Deer are scary. Have you ever taken a good look at their teeth and those pointy hooves? And, if that wasn't enough, most of them have sharp horns on their heads just to poke wolves!" Dolt closed his eyes and shuddered at the thought of the dangerous deer while Blood Warrior rolled his eyes.

Tasha turned to Dolt and said in a comforting manner, "What do you eat? How do you stay alive?"

Dolt slowly rose to his feet but hung his head. "I eat plants... and berries when I can find them."

Tasha asked, "Would you eat deer meat if someone killed it for you?"

Before Dolt could answer, Blood Warrior exploded, "What? Tasha, you've got to be kidding me! Who ever heard of having to feed a grown wolf?"

Tasha began to nuzzle and lick Blood Warrior, "Honey, there's probably not another wolf big and strong enough to do that except for you. You are the greatest hunter of all time. It would be nothing for you to kill enough game to feed one more mouth."

Blood Warrior complained, "Father Wolf, Tasha! You do this to me any the time you want something. I know what you're doing!"

Tasha ignored his protest and continued to stroke his ego. "Honey, I don't know what you're talking about. I do know that you are such a great hunter, you could kill enough game to feed ten wolves. You could feed one more wolf if you hunted on just three legs!"

Blood Warrior looked into her penetrating blue eyes. He knew he could never deny her anything that she wanted. He turned to Dolt. "Okay, I'm going to allow you to join our pack, but the minute you start being to be too much trouble, you're gone!" Dolt gave a grateful nod of his head.

Within an hour, Blood Warrior stalked and killed a buck deer. Tasha had stayed behind with the fearful Dolt. When Blood Warrior dropped the carcass at their feet, Dolt immediately backed away, trembling. Tasha barked reassuringly, "Don't be afraid. The deer is dead. It can't hurt you."

Dolt whined, "Are you sure? Those horns look awfully sharp."

Tasha nudged the dead deer, "See, it's dead. Now, come eat. We need to get some meat on your bones."

Blood Warrior blinked his eyes to make sure they weren't playing tricks on him as he thought, *Dear Father Wolf! Surely, this can't be happening. This can't be real.* Dolt took his first tentative bite, slowly chewed the meat and finally swallowed. Tasha said excitedly, "See there! See how good that tastes! Good job, Dolt!" Tasha and Blood Warrior did not feed until Dolt's stomach was full. Tasha, because she wanted to encourage Dolt. Blood Warrior, because the whole scene was almost too ludicrous to believe.

Over the next few months, the trio of wolves successfully hunted, with Blood Warrior and Tasha making all the kills. Dolt continued to put on weight. He now weighed almost 100 pounds and his coat had lost its dull, straw-like quality and began to shine.

Dolt was becoming bolder but there were still plenty of incidents where he showed his cravenness. Once, a crow suddenly cawed from a nearby tree, causing Dolt to jump sideways and submissively slink to the ground. Blood Warrior shook his head and muttered under his breath, "Father Wolf in the Sky."

When they were hunting, Blood Warrior would usually be in the lead with Tasha by his side or right behind him. Dolt timidly brought up the rear, while constantly darting his eyes in all directions watching for danger. One time, while hunting, the wolves froze when they heard the raspy yelps of hen turkeys followed by the full-throated gobbles of the males.

Blood Warrior softly said, "All three of us will stalk these turkeys. Dolt, this means you too. It's time you started pulling your own weight in this pack. We must be quiet and careful. Turkeys have excellent eyesight and hearing. If the damn things could smell, we'd never kill one of them." Dolt's eyes said he was panic-stricken. Tasha nuzzled him reassuringly. "You can do this. I believe in you."

The wolves snuck within killing distance of the flock. Blood Warrior softly said, "Now," and they rushed the birds. Blood Warrior and Tasha leapt high in the air to each bring down a fat turkey as they tried to fly off. Dolt had not budged. He had just stood there, shaking with fright. The wolves quickly broke the necks of the turkeys. The dead birds lay still on the forest floor. Suddenly, one of the turkeys began a dying quiver as his wings thumped against the leaves where he lay.

Dolt's first thought was the turkey had faked his death and this was part of a premeditated plot to kill the wolves. Dolt yipped, terrified, "Yikes! He's after me!" He turned with his tail tucked between his legs and fled as fast as he could run.

Blood Warrior began laughing hysterically. Tasha shot him a disapproving look as she ran after Dolt. She chased him for almost a mile before she could get him slowed down enough to see the turkey was not after him.

Dolt sheepishly looked at Tasha. "Why do you put up with me? I am a worthless coward. I am such a liability to you and Blood Warrior." Dolt hung his head.

Tasha nuzzled and licked the craven wolf. "Dolt, you've got to stop that. You have got to start having a higher opinion of yourself. Quit putting yourself down all the time. Now come on. Let's go eat some of that tasty turkey. Have you ever eaten turkey?"

Dolt brightened. "Once, when I was just being weaned from my mother's teat. She brought my litter a turkey that she had killed. I do remember that it was good!"

When Tasha and Dolt rejoined Blood Warrior, all three began to feed on the turkeys. As he ate, Dolt kept a wary eye on the turkey carcasses, making sure they didn't come back to life to exact their revenge.

Blood Warrior was surprised to find that he was developing an affection for Dolt. When Tasha noticed it, she was even more surprised. Dolt was the most surprised of all when he sensed that Blood Warrior did not hate him, but for some inexplicable reason actually liked him.

While much of the new territory was the same as the old one, there was one big difference: geysers. Blood Warrior had learned about the eruptions of boiling hot water and steam the hard way after being sprayed by a small random geyser.

The minor scalding caused him to learn to recognize the openings or vents of the volcanic heated water spouts. Blood Warrior noticed there was one geyser that erupted the exact same time each day. It shot 8,000 gallons of boiling water at over 250 degrees temperature, 150 feet into the air in a matter of just a couple of minutes. Being in the general area of the geysers always caused Blood Warrior's nose to wrinkle in disgust at the stink created by hydrogen sulfide gas, which was a by-product of the geysers.

BLOOD
WARRIOR
RETURNS

One night, Tasha overheard Blood Warrior muttering to himself, *"Demon, Glutton, Talon, Sly, Red Fang and his entire pack."* Tasha said, "Honey, I know who those creatures are because you have told me how they massacred your family, but why are you saying their names?"

Blood Warrior responded, "I say their names every night because I want to keep fresh in my mind what they did to my family." He continued, "One day, I will go back to my old home and settle the score for my father, mother, brothers and sisters."

Tasha thought about what Blood Warrior had said for several days. Finally, she asked Blood Warrior, "When do you want to go home?"

He was surprised, "Well, I'm not sure..." When he didn't finish what he was going to say, Tasha barked, "You are hesitant because you don't know what to do with me and Dolt, aren't you?"

Blood Warrior responded, "No, it's not exactly that..."

She barked a little louder, "Of course it is! That's exactly why you haven't gone back. You know it's dangerous and you don't want to put us in harm's way."

He answered, "Tasha, if something happened to you, I would not want to live."

Tasha responded, "Well, I feel the same way about you! My place is with you. If you die, I die. But, this is something you must do. I understand that. I think you should do it, too. I feel that your family is also my family. I want them avenged. When do we leave?"

After a week of carefully considering all the possible outcomes that might result from his returning home, Blood Warrior nuzzled Tasha and softly barked, "I am ready to go home. I agree that you should go with me but we will have to leave Dolt here."

Tasha licked his jaw, "I'm ready when you are. We should tell Dolt."

When Blood Warrior explained their plans and the necessity of leaving him here, Dolt protested. "No! I want to go too! I can fight now! You have given me the courage!"

Blood Warrior explained, "Dolt, this is serious business. Deadly serious. We will be fighting grizzlies, wolverines, eagles, cougars and an outlaw wolf pack. You can't come. I won't be able to protect you."

Dolt begged, "Please, Blood Warrior, take me with you. When I met you and Tasha, I was a total and complete failure. I was slowly starving myself to death. Without the two of you,

I would already be dead by now. I would rather die defending you and Tasha than go back to the slow death of my old life."

Blood Warrior looked at Tasha. She shrugged because she didn't know what to do with Dolt either. After thinking about it for a few minutes, Blood Warrior warned, "You can go, but you need to understand that you might be killed for your trouble."

Dolt wagged his tail and grinned, "Yesss!" Secretly, Dolt hoped that Blood Warrior and Tasha could not read his mind. He was still terrified of going with them but he was even more afraid of being left alone.

Blood Warrior, Tasha and Dolt began the journey back to Blood Warrior's home territory the next morning. They were careful to communicate in soft barks with absolutely no howling. They didn't want his enemies alerted that Blood Warrior was back until he was ready to reveal himself to them. Blood Warrior didn't take the fastest direct route, but traveled in a zigzag fashion, sticking to the heaviest cover.

When they finally reached familiar territory, Blood Warrior smiled as he heard the chatter of a squirrel insulting a quail, "Dear Father Squirrel in the Sky! Can't you say anything besides 'bob...white'? Bob...white, bob...white, bob...white! You're driving anyone else with half a brain nuts! Come up with a new line once in a while! How about bark...y, bark...y, bark...y?"

The dim-witted quail responded, "Bob...white!"

Barky disgustedly shrieked, "Squirrel shit!!!!"

In spite of the need to be as quiet as possible, Blood Warrior couldn't help but to laugh loudly. "I was hoping that you were smart enough to come up with some new insults while I was gone. That's what I get for hoping."

For once in his life, Barky was speechless at the sight of the giant timber wolf and the two strange wolves. When he finally found his voice, Barky marveled at the size of the huge timber wolf, squeaking, "What the hell happened to you? You used to be a little coyote!"

Blood Warrior replied, "Well, I found a forest infested with squirrels. After I ate about a thousand of them, I grew to this size."

Barky sputtered with laughter, "Blood Warrior, my friend, it is good to see you back. Who are your companions?"

Blood Warrior made the introductions. "This is my mate, Tasha, and that is Dolt." Blood Warrior gave Barky a look and a slight shake of his head that said to leave Dolt alone. Instead, Barky focused on Tasha. "Tasha, is this overgrown coyote the best you can do? A good-looking wolf like you should have her pick of mates. Is there something wrong with your eyesight?"

Tasha was already giggling because of what had already been said, plus Blood Warrior had told her all about Barky. "My mate is handsome, but you do kind of have to squint a little bit."

Barky chuckled. "I like her, Blood Warrior! She's going to fit right in!"

Blood Warrior turned serious as his demeanor darkened. "Barky, I do need your help. I need you to keep me informed of the whereabouts of Demon, Glutton, Talon, Sly and Red Fang. It is time they answered for slaughtering my family!"

Barky chattered, "I will do everything I can to help you, my friend. I think I have a good idea of what you've got in mind, but Blood Warrior, you cannot kill them all. You are the biggest timber wolf I've ever seen, but you are still no match for a grizzly bear or a wolf pack that has you outnumbered six to one. That's just plain suicide!"

Blood Warrior sat on his haunches and looked up at Barky, "I have had a lot of time to think about this. I believe I *can* kill them all, but it needs to be done one at a time and with the right plan. First, let's start with Glutton. Please find him for me."

IT BEGINS

I t took Barky half a day to locate Glutton. Glutton had discovered a killdeer's nest and was plundering the eggs. The mother killdeer chirped, "Kill...dee, kill...dee" as she was dragging a wing, pretending to be injured to lure Glutton away from her nest, but Glutton was not fooled. As Glutton greedily devoured the eggs, the brown-winged, white-bellied bird protested noisily, but to no avail. She would have to start over to try to make another family.

Barky glided back to Blood Warrior's hideout deep in a dense thicket, "I found Glutton! Do you want me to take you to him?"

Blood Warrior barked, "Yes, we will be ready to travel in just a minute." He turned to Tasha and Dolt to give them their instructions. "Don't be fooled by his relatively small size. The wolverine is fast and much stronger than he looks. Glutton is very dangerous. I will be the one who will fight him. Both of you stay out of it. There will be others that I will need your help with, but not this one."

Blood Warrior continued, "Barky, let's go." To the other two wolves, he quietly announced, "And now, *it begins*."

The squirrel and the three wolves moved silently through the forest. They arrived in time to see Glutton, having caught the mother killdeer, swallowing what was left of her. Feathers were scattered on the ground and a few were stuck to his lips.

The wolverine's eyes grew large at the sight of the giant black wolf with the golden eyes. He noticed two other wolves circling out to the side. Blood Warrior growled, "What's the matter wolverine? Don't you recognize me? You killed my sisters. Today, you have to answer for that!"

Glutton finally recognized Blood Warrior. A feeling of dread swept over Glutton as his confidence was shaken by his worst nightmare. He whimpered fearfully, "Now wait a minute! That wasn't my fault! I was just defending myself!"

Blood Warrior snarled, "My father told me that you even licked the last of their blood from the ground! Today your blood will pay for the blood of my sisters!"

Glutton realized by the look in Blood Warrior's eyes that begging was a waste of time. He arched his back and bristled his fur. "Many wolves before you have made the mistake of underestimating me. This poor judgment on your part will cost you your life just like it did with your stupid sisters!" Out of desperation, Glutton bared his razor sharp teeth and with lightning quickness lunged at Blood Warrior's throat. Blood Warrior matched his quickness by sidestepping the charge and throwing a shoulder into the wolverine, knocking him down.

Blood Warrior leapt on his back and sank his teeth into the back of Glutton's neck and shook him. Glutton cried, "Stop!

Let go! You're killing me! Please... stop!" Blood Warrior tightened his grip until he could hear the snap of Glutton's neck.

Barky provided the running commentary. "Now what, Glutton? I thought you claimed to be some type of badass! Where you at? What's up? Just like I thought, you ain't shit!"

Blood Warrior gave Glutton's carcass a couple more shakes for good measure, then dropped the dead wolverine in a disjointed heap. He desperately wanted to give a victory howl but kept himself in check. Blood Warrior saw Dolt throw back his head to howl but silenced him. "Be quiet! We have much more work to do before my family is avenged. I don't want any of my enemies warned before the time when they have to answer to me."

Tasha nuzzled and licked Blood Warrior. "It's funny. I thought I would be afraid for you but I wasn't afraid at all. Somehow, I knew you would kill him. Even though he had killed wolves before, the wolverine was no match for you."

Dolt chimed in, "Yeah, me too. I wasn't scared at all." The other two wolves knew it was a lie. They had seen the fear in his eyes. Blood Warrior and Tasha felt Dolt was making progress. Even though he was lying, Dolt previously would have announced to one and all what a craven he was. It was a shaky step, but a step nonetheless in the right direction.

Barky chattered excitedly, "I told that dumb-ass he was going down! Maybe some of these animals will listen to me now!"

Blood Warrior cautioned him, "Barky, I know this is going to be hard for you but you can't tell anybody yet what happened here."

Barky sputtered, "But, can't I at least tell…"

Blood Warrior cut him off. "No one, Barky! No one!"

Barky sighed. "Squirrel shit! This is the best news ever and I can't say anything. Okay, I won't say anything but I don't have to like it!" Barky stuck his tongue out at Blood Warrior. Tasha began to laugh at the comical look on Barky's face. She was quickly followed by Dolt, then Blood Warrior. Finally even Barky joined the contagious laughter.

When the hunting party left the body of Glutton to scavengers, the only witness was a red-headed woodpecker who drummed out his delight on a dead tree limb at the death of the hated wolverine.

FACING TALON

The three wolves spent the next few days hidden in one of the many thickets deep in the forest. They hunted at night, dragging their kills back to their hideout. They made sure they ate everything to help reduce any tell-tale blood smell. When the wolves were finished with a kill, the only things left were skulls, horns and hooves. Occasionally, they would hear the howls of other wolves but did not answer them. It chafed Blood Warrior to hide. It went against his nature.

In a few days, Blood Warrior asked Barky, "Would you be willing to help me on the next kill? I have to warn you, it will be dangerous."

Barky hesitated. "Well... what would I have to do?"

Blood Warrior grimly replied, "You would be the bait to bring Talon in close enough so I can kill him."

Barky took several minutes to mull the concept over. "On one paw, I don't much like the idea of being bait. On the other paw, the biggest threat to my life is that damn eagle. It would be nice to eliminate him. What exactly would I have to do?"

Blood Warrior said, "You would have to pretend to be injured. That would require you to be on the ground and

I know you don't like that." Barky blew air out of the gap between his two front teeth, closed his eyes and thought about it before continuing, "Well, I would have to know a helluva lot more of what you have in mind."

Blood Warrior stalked back and forth a few times, sat down and said, "I would be in hiding. The plan would be for me to catch and kill Talon before he gets to you. It would require perfect timing on my part. Frankly, it depends on how much you trust me. If you don't want to do it, I understand completely. If I were in your position I'm not sure I would do it."

Barky's little face was scrunched up with worry. "Let me think about it for a day or two."

Later, when the wolves were alone with Dolt listening intently, Tasha softly barked, "Honey, you know I think you can do anything, but can you really pull this off? It sounds really dangerous for Barky and for you."

Blood Warrior responded, "It is dangerous. Very dangerous. I wanted to make sure Barky understood that. I also know that you have great confidence in me, especially when you want something!"

Tasha yipped, "Honey!" and gave Blood Warrior a playful little nip.

Barky did not wait long but came back the next day. "I'm probably the dumbest squirrel who ever lived, but it's worth the risk. I'm tired of always craning my neck, looking for Talon. I am going to trust you, my friend."

That night the wolves and the squirrel crept within sight of the tree that held Talon's nest. Before they left, Blood Warrior told Tasha and Dolt, "This is another time where I won't need your help unless my plan goes wrong. Then, you need to come running."

Tasha and Dolt took cover deep in a thicket as they laid down and did not move. Blood Warrior crawled through the thicket to the edge of the clearing and silently buried himself under the leaves. He slowed down his breathing so there was no tell-tale movement of the leaves.

At dawn, Barky initiated the plan by pretending to fall from a nearby tree, crawling to where Blood Warrior was hidden. When he got within a few feet of Blood Warrior, he turned on his back, kicking and crying as if mortally wounded.

Talon had watched this whole farce from his nest. He thought, *This is going to be a great day! It's starting out with breakfast in bed!* Blood Warrior watched the eagle leave his nest and begin the dive for the easy meal. As Talon set his wings to brake a few feet from the ground, Blood Warrior exploded out of the leaves and grabbed the eagle by the neck. Blood Warrior knew that he had to kill the eagle quickly or be disemboweled by his sharp claws. The big wolf viciously bit off the eagle's head and danced away from the frantic clutching of the murderous claws.

As Blood Warrior cautiously watched the dying flutters of Talon, Tasha and Dolt burst out of hiding. Tasha ran to Barky, "Are you okay? Are you hurt?"

Barky replied, "The son of a bitch didn't touch me, but damn him, he made me crap all over myself!" Tasha started giggling and soon the three wolves and the squirrel were prostrate on the forest floor, laughing uproariously. When they gained their composure, Barky, as was his wont, could not leave without having the last word. He backed up to the eagle's carcass, lifted his tail and farted on the remains. The wolves, already slaphappy, dissolved into another round of laughter.

As they left the headless body of Talon in the dirt, the news of his death spread throughout the bird kingdom. As the sun shone brightly, over a hundred birds of various species gathered on the limbs of the surrounding pine and aspen trees, chirping and singing happy songs of celebration over the body of the dreaded and deadly Talon.

When the wolves got back to their hideout and all began to doze and nap, Tasha heard Blood Warrior mutter softly in his sleep, "Demon, Sly, Red Fang."

SLY'S TURN

Killing Glutton and Talon had been relatively easy for Blood Warrior. He was physically superior to the wolverine and the eagle. The next killer whom he marked for death was Sly. This was going to require a lot more thought because the cougar was stronger and faster than the wolves—even Blood Warrior.

Blood Warrior asked Barky to locate Sly. Blood Warrior said to Tasha and Dolt, "I know I've kept you out of the action so far, but this time I will need your help in killing the cougar."

Tasha bared her teeth and growled, "I am ready to fight! What do you need me to do?"

Dolt put up a brave (but false) front. His voice broke as he half growled and half squeaked, "I am ready too."

Blood Warrior looked on Tasha with confidence and on Dolt with skepticism. "We will have to fight Sly as a team. She is extremely dangerous. When we confront her, we must circle her continually. If we become stationary, she will kill us. We also have to keep equal spacing around her. We have to have her vulnerable from an attack from the rear at all times. Dolt, you are crucial to our success. Sly will have a much harder job protecting herself from three wolves instead of two." Dolt swallowed hard trying to keep the fear from welling up in him. He stifled the desire to turn and run.

When Barky located Sly, he led the wolves to where she was lying on an elevated rock overlooking a small valley. As they approached her, Blood Warrior growled, "You better get your scared ass up a tree or we will kill you." He was trying to use her pride against her. They would have no chance to kill her if she took to the trees.

Sly smirked. "Funny, that's what your dumb brother said to me right before I killed him. By the way, he was delicious. I don't need to run from wolves. It is a simple matter for me to kill you. You are the one who needs to climb a tree to live." Sly laughed. "Of course, you weaklings couldn't climb a tree if your lives depended on it. And your lives do depend on it, so get ready to die!"

As the wolves circled her, the cougar kept whirling around, protecting her blind side. Dolt was starting to falter as his circles became larger and larger, trying to put more distance between himself and Sly. Blood Warrior saw an opening and struck at one of her hind legs. His powerful jaws crushed the bone. Sly whirled and slashed Blood Warrior with the claws from one of her front legs. Her claws ripped the flesh in his shoulder, knocking him down. Sly followed up her advantage, attacking the downed wolf.

Tasha yelped, "No!" and sprung to his defense. Sly abandoned her strike against Blood Warrior and focused on Tasha. In spite of her courageous fight, Sly got Tasha by the throat and started to tighten the killing bite.

When the fighting started, Dolt had steadily backed away in fright. When he saw his beloved Tasha, who had been so kind to him, in the death grip of the big cat, his long suppressed instincts took over as he bared his teeth and launched himself at Sly. Dolt sank his teeth into the back of the cougar's neck. Dolt snarled through clenched teeth, "Turn her loose! Turn her loose!" Sly let go of Tasha as Sly squirmed and twisted, trying to get the wolf off her neck and back. In spite of her violent gyrations, Dolt stubbornly kept his grip on her neck. Blood Warrior got back on his feet and joined the fray. He managed to penetrate her defenses and bit down on her throat. Blood Warrior had Sly by the front and Dolt had her by the back. Together they crunched the life out of her.

When the big cougar was finally dead, Tasha rushed up to Dolt. "You saved my life! That's one of the bravest things I've ever seen!"

Blood Warrior added, "Yes, you were incredibly brave. As the pack leader, I have the authority to change your name. You will no longer be called Dolt. Your new name is Valor!" For the first time in his life, Valor knew what it felt like to be proud of himself.

They didn't walk away unscathed. Blood Warrior had gaping scratches on his shoulder and Tasha had deep teeth marks on her neck. They had to lay up and rest for a week to heal and recover. Valor continued to grow as a wolf. He went out on his own and brought a deer back to his injured pack mates. As Blood Warrior and Tasha feasted on the deer, Blood Warrior offered congratulations. "Good job, Valor. I couldn't have done a better job myself!" Valor puffed up with pride from being praised for his hunting ability and being compared favorably to Blood Warrior, whom he worshiped.

Blood Warrior had now engineered the deaths of Glutton, Talon and Sly. While their deaths were major accomplishments, none of them were on a level of killing the monster grizzly bear or the rogue wolf pack. To kill them would require his keenest strategy and the help of everyone he could enlist.

DESTROYING
DEMON

———————

Blood Warrior knew that, for the most part, the first three killings had gone off without too many complications. Any complications on the next two targets would probably result in the deaths of himself, Tasha, Valor and Barky. Blood Warrior prayed. *Father Wolf, thank you for being with me as I avenged the murders of my family. I need you more than ever now. Please continue to be with me and bless me as I seek to bring justice for my family.*

Blood Warrior chose to go after Demon next. He began to plot what seemed to be an impossible task. How could a 300 pound wolf kill a 2,000 pound grizzly bear?

The day that Blood Warrior sent Barky to locate Demon, it put all the wolves' nerves on edge. Tasha anxiously barked, "Honey, what is your plan?" When Blood Warrior explained his plan to Tasha and Valor, their eyes widened in wonder and disbelief. Tasha responded, "Honey, that sounds crazy, but I have total confidence in you. If you say it will work, I'm in!"

Valor nudged Blood Warrior, "You are not only my pack leader but you are also my friend. Anything you need from me, you've got it!"

Blood Warrior nodded his head in appreciation to the two wolves. He couldn't help but have his doubts about Valor. *He showed his courage by coming to the rescue of Tasha, but I wonder if he would do the same for me?*

Barky returned with the news of Demon's location. "I found him! Are you sure about this? Do you remember how big he is?"

Blood Warrior barked, "I remember how big he is, but he has to answer for Ulrich and Aiyana! Please take me to him!"

When the three wolves approached Demon, the huge grizzly roared as he snapped his teeth together. "I recognize you, Blood Warrior. It's nice to see that you've put some meat on your bones. That's the way I like my wolves—the meatier the better!"

Blood Warrior bristled as he growled, "Today is the day I settle with you over the deaths of my brother and my sister."

Demon roared with laughter, "Are you crazy? Have you actually come to challenge me to fight? You will be dead in the time it would take to shut my jaws!"

Blood Warrior knew one of the keys to his plan was to get Demon angry enough to follow him. He started by insulted Demon. "I've never breathed a day in my life that I couldn't beat a big, fat, slow piece of shit like you! If you've got any grizzly bear buddies, you better go get them because you're going to need them."

Demon's beady, pig-like eyes flamed red with anger as he charged Blood Warrior, roaring and snapping his teeth. Tasha and Valor had kept their distance as Blood Warrior had instructed them to. The three wolves dashed away to avoid Demon's murderous charge. They had to be very careful as grizzly bears are incredibly fast for short periods of time. Blood Warrior had gauged his distance to Demon to allow himself enough space to be able to get safely away from any attack.

Try as he might, Demon could not cut down the distance that separated him and the wolves. When he finally stopped, he was out of breath as he panted, "What the hell? I thought you wanted to fight! You made all these big threats and then you run like a coward!"

Blood Warrior turned and grinned from a safe distance, "Sorry, but I don't quite feel it yet! I need a special feeling to give you the ass-whipping you deserve!"

Barky had followed them, gliding from tree to tree. He was also fully versed in Blood Warrior's plan as he joined in the insults, "Hey lard-ass! You look like you're about to die! I'd been willing to bet my entire winter's stock of nuts that the wolf kicks your fat butt!"

The chase went off and on for almost three hours as Demon continued pursuing the wolves. Anytime he seemed like he might abandon the pursuit, the three wolves and the squirrel would chide and insult him enough to keep him going by stoking his anger.

Blood Warrior kept checking the sun. He knew his timing would have to be perfect for his plan to work. Blood Warrior smiled when he smelled the sulfur. Usually he hated the smell. Today he loved it. He thought, *I hope this geyser stays faithful to its regular eruption.*

When he had Demon positioned perfectly, Blood Warrior quit running and began to circle him. In accordance with the plan, Tasha and Valor also started circling the bear. As they began to make feints at Demon, he stood on his hind legs to fight them with powerful swats from his paws. "Come on, you cowardly bunch of wolves! Who wants to be the first one to feel my claws and my teeth?"

Blood Warrior heard the familiar rumbling noise that came right before an eruption. At the predetermined signal, Blood Warrior shouted to the other two wolves, "Run!"

The big grizzly stood his ground, confused as to why the wolves were acting so strangely. Demon was unfamiliar with the territory and he had never seen a geyser, much less straddled one. His world turned into horrific pain and then to blackness. Demon was given a high-pressure, 250-degree enema that parboiled him on the spot.

When the geyser subsided, the wolves went out to check on the cooked bear. Black smoke rolled off what was left of the bear's body. The smell of burnt flesh was overwhelming. The boiling water had peeled the fur off of Demon. He was now unrecognizable as a grizzly bear.

Barky chattered from a distant tree, "Holy squirrel shit! I would have never believed it if I hadn't seen it! Blood Warrior, remind me to never doubt you again. If you tell me you can fly, I'm going to start building you a nest!"

With Demon dead, Blood Warrior was ready to leave the geyser country. He had never been comfortable there. It was not home. He and his pack headed for home.

RED FANG REVENGE

Blood Warrior, Tasha, Valor and even Barky rested for a few weeks. Blood Warrior thought that by now Red Fang suspected something was up. Blood Warrior knew that the killings of Glutton, Talon, Sly and Demon were big news in the animal kingdom. It was all the animals were talking about. Even though wolf tracks were evident at each of the kill scenes, no one knew which wolves were responsible. No one had heard any howls of victory, which was odd for wolves. Most speculation centered on Red Fang. Of course, Red Fang knew he wasn't responsible.

Blood Warrior thought, *Now I have to think of a way to kill fifteen wolves. And not just ordinary wolves—wolves that are completely crazy and will do whatever they're told by Red Fang without question. I cannot kill them as a pack. I have to plan a way to separate them into smaller groups. I can deal with them three or four at a time.*

Red Fang told Brutus and Adolph, "Our pack seems to be getting the credit for the killings of Glutton, Talon, Sly and Demon, but we know we didn't do it. The question is: who did do it?"

Brutus responded, "It has to be an animal at least as powerful as a cougar."

Adolph interjected, "Idiot, there were no cougar tracks at the kill sites, only wolf tracks."

Brutus argued, "So, are you telling me there is some kind of super wolf or wolves killing these assholes?"

As the mentally challenged brothers continued their argument, Red Fang thought to himself, *I may have made a mistake by not hunting down and killing the only surviving son of Thunder. What was his name? Oh yeah, Blood Warrior. Could he be the wolf behind these killings? Thunder was an above-average wolf, but nothing really special. Certainly not in my class. I don't know why his son would be any different. But I don't like someone operating in my territory when I know nothing about them. I think I will send out scouting parties to get to the bottom of this.*

The next morning, Red Fang sent out scouting parties consisting of three wolves each. He did not select his best fighters as he didn't think it would require much to go look and report back what they'd seen. When the three surveillance parties left in different directions, they had an unseen observer.

Being quiet was difficult for Barky. It took everything within him to keep his mouth shut, but he had promised Blood Warrior that he would keep an eye on Red Fang and his pack. Blood Warrior had asked him to report any suspicious activity.

By chance, one of the parties was headed in the direction of Blood Warrior's hideout. Barky managed to skirt the three wolves without being seen or heard. He continued gliding from tree to tree as fast as he could. When Barky reached the hideout, he chattered, "They're coming, three of Red Fang's wolves!"

The lounging wolves snapped to attention. Blood Warrior asked, "Where are they?"

Barky responded as he pointed his paw, "They are quite a distance in that direction."

Blood Warrior said, "I wonder what they're doing?"

Barky replied, "Unless I miss my guess, they are looking for you."

The worst of Red Fang's inbred imbeciles couldn't remember their own names so Red Fang assigned them numbers. The three wolves in this scouting party were #2, #6 and #11. They could follow orders but were lost when it came to thinking for themselves.

Blood Warrior set an ambush for them. He instructed Tasha and Valor to follow his lead. Blood Warrior wasn't sure exactly what he was going to do when he confronted them but he felt confident that he could adjust to the situation.

Blood Warrior stepped out from behind a lodgepole pine directly in the path of the three wolves. All three wolves skidded to a stop and began snarling. #2 growled, "Who are you?"

Blood Warrior retorted, "That depends. Who are you looking for?"

#11 jumped in. "We're looking for... what was his name again?"

#6 added, "I think Red Fang said... Blind... Blind... something or other." The three wolves began to argue among themselves as to the name of the object of their search. They finally came into agreement. #2 asked Blood Warrior, "Are you Blind Wartfrog?"

Even though Barky knew he was supposed to be quiet and be just an observer, he began to snicker. Their stupidity was comical but that didn't make them any less dangerous. In fact it made them even more dangerous. They didn't perceive risk or danger like normal wolves. They were oblivious to potential hazards. It had the net effect of making them fearless. Also, their mental capabilities, or lack thereof, had no bearing on their physical development. They were big, strong and vicious.

Blood Warrior realized this was an opportunity to pare down Red Fang's pack and reduce the horrendous odds stacked against him from coming out on top in the struggle with the renegade wolf. He asked the closest wolf, "Do you mean Blood Warrior?"

#2 responded, "Well...yes...yes...I believe that's it! That's the bad wolf's name!"

Blood Warrior was thinking that this was almost too easy. "And if you found this bad wolf, what did Red Fang want you to do?"

#11 butted in. "We're supposed to go back to Red Fang and tell him where the bad wolf is."

Blood Warrior almost felt sorry for them but remembered these three played a part in the murder and mutilation of his family. They had mercilessly ripped his family into pieces. Another factor was they needed to be taken out of the gene pool. Blood Warrior thought, *Father Wolf, help us all if these three idiots were to breed and produce even more idiotic children!*

Blood Warrior softly barked, "Now." With that, Tasha and Valor sprang out from hiding and joined Blood Warrior in the attack on the wolves. Blood Warrior immediately knocked #2 down and seized him by the throat.

#2 threatened, "Let go of me! My father will kill you!"

Blood Warrior growled, "Not today, he won't!" As he choked the life out of the snarling, thrashing wolf, he checked on the welfare of Tasha and Valor.

Tasha had the upper hand on #11 and already had her on her back with a death grip on her throat.

#11 whimpered, "Please stop. You are hurting me."

Tasha snarled as she tightened her grip, "You weren't so concerned about hurting my mate's family when you and your pack were murdering them!" #11's body shuddered and went limp in death.

Valor was not faring well. Blood was flowing from several bites and Valor was slowly retreating under #6's savage attack.

#6 gloated, "How does it feel being killed? You will be dead soon."

Valor fought back. "I am not dead yet."

Blood Warrior whirled to help Valor. Valor was fighting hard but was almost on his back when Blood Warrior jumped on #6's back and sank his teeth into his neck. #6 yelped and desperately tried to dislodge Blood Warrior. "Quit, you coward! It's two against one!" With one forceful crunch, Blood Warrior broke his neck.

Tasha rushed up to the exhausted Valor and began licking his wounds. "Are you all right?"

Valor croaked, "I think I'm okay, but these bites hurt! You and Blood Warrior won your fights pretty easily. I guess I'm a failure as a fighter."

Blood Warrior lied, "No, not at all. You were just unlucky to draw the biggest, meanest and toughest of the three. I should have realized that and engaged him first."

RAGE AND REPRISAL

B lood Warrior and his two-member pack went back into hiding to allow Valor time to heal. He moved their hideout to a spot deeper into the forest. Blood Warrior frequently went on scouting trips to check on the whereabouts of Red Fang and his pack. Barky did yeoman's service as a sentinel. Between the two, they made sure that they weren't surprised by the renegade wolves. Tasha went hunting by herself as Valor was too weak from his wounds and Blood Warrior was busy with reconnaissance. Killing enough game for all three was not a difficult task for her as she was extremely fast and very smart. She was able to keep all of them well fed.

When #2, #6 and #11 did not return to the pack, Red Fang combined the other two parties that had returned and sent the six wolves out to find the missing three. When the search and rescue group came back, they had grim news to report as #1 barked, "We found them but they're all dead!"

Red Fang flew into a blasphemous rage. "Damn you Father Wolf! Why have you betrayed me? I know this has to be the work of that damn Blood Warrior! Why did You let him live to vex me?" Red Fang howled, "I know it's you, Blood Warrior! I am going to kill you just as I killed your spineless father, your slutty mother and your sniveling brother and sisters! You will end up just like them, in small pieces!"

The rest of the wolves in his pack gave him a wide berth for a few days. They had seen his murderous temper before. Even the most simpleminded of them knew Red Fang would kill without cause or provocation. He might kill them just because he felt like it.

The tracks at the kill site told Red Fang that there were three wolves. One was hurt badly enough that there was a blood trail. Despite his attempt to track them, he failed when their spoor ended at a wide, rushing river.

Red Fang split his pack in two. He took one band, and put Adolph and Brutus in charge of the other. Red Fang's band went several miles up the river, and Adolph and Brutus's band went down the river. They meticulously searched both sides of the river but found nothing. It was as if Blood Warrior and the other two wolves had disappeared.

Red Fang flew into a rage as he bit every pack member that he could reach. "You bunch of worthless pieces of coyote shit! How any of you could be related to me is a mystery! Your sorry mothers must have been humping coyotes to get you bunch of brainless assholes! I give you one little thing to do and you can't do it!" His followers fled in a panic.

Barky was instrumental in helping his friends evade Red Fang. After directing them to wade in the river for over a mile, Barky chattered to Blood Warrior, "See that tree branch hanging low over the water?"

Blood Warrior replied, "I see it. So, what am I supposed to do with it?"

Barky shook his head in exasperation, "You're supposed to climb up on it! Are all wolves this dim-witted?"

Blood Warrior asked, "Have you lost your little mind, squirrel? Wolves do not climb trees unless it's an emergency."

Barky exploded, "Do you think being hunted by a pack of psychotic wolves would qualify as an emergency? Father Squirrel, help me!"

After all three wolves had clamored out of the water onto the thick limb and shook the water from their fur, Blood Warrior chided Barky, "Okay Super Squirrel, now what?"

Barky responded, "Now, you follow me." Barky led them up the limb to the trunk where there was another limb that led to the next tree.

Tasha laughed in delight. "Barky, you are brilliant! We are traveling from tree to tree and leaving no scent on the ground to follow!"

Blood Warrior had to grudgingly admit that it was a good idea but still grumbled, "Wolves were never meant to climb trees." Valor didn't say anything but there was a little white around his eyes as he was concerned at being so high off the ground.

When they got to a point that they were far enough away from the river that they could get down without being concerned that they could be followed, the wolves jumped to the ground.

Barky stayed in the tree. He rose up on his hind legs and waved his front paws in the air over his head. He pretended to be acknowledging the praises of a large crowd. "Thank you! Thank you, my friends! Please, you are too kind! Please, hold your praise! You are embarrassing me!"

The wolves could not help but to laugh at the preening squirrel. Finally, Blood Warrior barked, "Barky, do you ever shit or do you just stay full of it all of the time?"

Red Fang called his scattered pack back together. The wolves reluctantly responded to his howl. They were afraid of coming back but were even more terrified of not following his command. When the other eleven wolves assembled, Red Fang barked, "We are going to get this bastard wolf and his two nitwits if it's the last thing we do!" Red Fang continued, "#1, #4, #7 and #10 will be one scouting party with #1 in charge. The other detail will be #3, #8, #12 and #14 with #8 in charge." Red Fang eyed his troops for a minute before fiercely growling, "Do NOT come back until you have killed them! If you come back without proof of their deaths, I will kill you! NOW GO!!"

#5 had been killed by Shadow, #9 by Digger. Thunder killed #13 and #15. This left Red Fang, Delilah, Adolph and Brutus as the only wolves left at the den. The remaining three wolves kept a respectful distance from the volatile Red Fang. They had seen many examples of his cruelty but had never seen him stay enraged for this long a period of time.

Blood Warrior, Tasha and Valor were diligent about watching for signs of Red Fang and his pack. They knew he would want to kill them even more now and was probably searching for them. Barky was a huge help keeping the surrounding countryside under surveillance for any trace of the marauders' whereabouts.

BARKY MEETS
HIS MATCH

It was not unusual to see other squirrels, but Barky harassed any strange squirrels to the point that they didn't hang around long. One day a new squirrel was seen in the trees. Barky immediately went to pester the new squirrel to make it feel not-at-home. But for one of the rare times in his life, Barky was struck speechless. He found himself gawking at a beautiful red female squirrel with a silken gray face and rich orange eyes.

All Barky could do was stare. Finally, she chattered as she returned his gaze, "Do you have a problem?"

Barky swallowed a couple of times and managed to squeak, "Problem?... No, there's no problem."

The female squirrel responded, "Well, put your eyes back in your head and tell me what you want."

Barky managed to croak, "What's your name?"

She tartly barked, "And, who wants to know?"

Barky said hoarsely, "My name is Barky."

The female tossed her head. "Barky is a dumb name for a squirrel. My name is Missy."

The two squirrels just looked at each other until Missy commanded, "Well don't just stand there with your mouth open, Bucky, say something!"

Barky chattered in a barely audible voice, "Barky."

Missy screwed up her face into a question mark, "What? I can't understand you. What are you saying? It sounds like you have a mouth full of pine nuts!"

Barky spoke louder, "Barky… my name is Barky, not Bucky."

Missy muttered, "Whatever."

Blood Warrior, Tasha and Valor could hear the squirrels' conversation. They looked up with their mouths hanging open. They had never seen Barky so meek and mild. All three wolves were so amazed that it was fortunate that Red Fang and his gang were not around as they were so distracted by the squirrel drama, they would have been easy prey for their enemies.

After a short time without them, Barky found his gonads along with his spine. "Missy, do you have a mate?"

Now it was Missy's turn to be speechless. Finally she sputtered, "What?…I can't believe… what do you think I am? Who do you think you are?"

Barky moved closer. "I am the answer to your prayers to Father Squirrel. I am the squirrel you always hoped you'd meet but were afraid you wouldn't. I am your mate and the future father of your pups!"

Missy had a coughing jag as she tried to regain her composure. "Bucky, you are completely insane! Have you lost your mind?"

Blood Warrior answered her from below. "Yes, he is crazier than a loon."

Barky sarcastically chattered down to the wolf, "Oh, I'm sorry. I didn't realize that I had asked for your help. But if I decide I ever need help, I will call on you first."

Until then Missy had not noticed the presence of the three wolves. She swiveled her head back and forth, looking at Barky then looking at the wolves. Missy said to Barky, "Do you know these wolves?"

Barky nodded his head. "Yes, they are my best friends. The big ugly one is Blood Warrior. The beautiful one is Tasha and the nice one is Valor."

Missy was incredulous. "You are friends with wolves?"

Barky grinned. "Sure, don't all squirrels have wolf friends?"

As Missy stared at them with wide eyes and an open mouth, Blood Warrior said, "Hi Missy, I'm glad to know you."

Tasha chimed in, "Hello Missy, I think you are the most beautiful squirrel that I've ever seen."

Valor added, "What's up?"

Missy gravely informed Barky, "I don't know if anyone has ever told you this, Bucky, but wolves *EAT* squirrels!"

Barky's whole body shook with a deep belly laugh. "I think I've heard rumors to that effect. *Some* wolves do eat *some* squirrels. *These* wolves won't eat *this* squirrel. As I've said, we're best friends. Now, quit changing the subject and quit calling me Bucky. My name is Barky. Do you want to be my mate?"

After swallowing hard a number of times, Missy was aghast. "Dear Father Squirrel, *NO!* Out of all the squirrels in the forest, you would be my last choice!"

Barky smirked at the wolves and winked. "She wants me!" Missy fled as fast as she could glide from tree to tree away from Barky. Barky pursued her, chattering, "Don't think I don't know that you're just putting on an act for my friends, pretending to run away!" Barky stopped momentarily and barked at the wolves, "Does she have a great sense of humor or what?" Barky then took off again, chasing the besieged Missy.

As the wolves watched the squirrels glide away, Tasha barked, "Hmmmm, Mr. Barky may have just met his match."

Blood Warrior snorted, "You don't know that! You females just have to stick together. All of you think you have the upper hand against the males."

Tasha nuzzled Blood Warrior. "Now honey, you know I'm just a female. Of course I don't know as much as you. You're the smartest and strongest wolf in the forest!"

Blood Warrior barked loudly, "Stop that, Tasha! Again, I know what you're doing! I'm not a complete idiot!"

Tasha licked his jaw and said with wide, innocent eyes, "I'm sure I don't know what you're talking about." Valor quietly chuckled as he knew better than to voice his opinion about Tasha's intentions.

Barky finally caught up with an exhausted Missy, landing on the same limb where Missy was gasping for air. Barky chuckled, "Missy, can we get serious for a minute? Can you imagine what our pups would be like if I was their father? They would be awesome!"

When Missy caught her breath, she chattered, "The thought of what our pups would be like is enough to cause me to pray to Father Squirrel to be barren!"

Barky laughed again. "I thought I was bad, but don't you ever get tired of cracking jokes?"

Missy gathered herself and with as much force as she could muster barked, "I am *NOT* joking, Bucky! When are you going to get that through that little, thick skull of yours?"

Their conversation was interrupted by the sound of the wind whistling through the wings of a Great Horned Owl. His talons were fully extended as he clutched for Missy. When Missy saw her impending doom, she screamed, "Help!"

Before the owl could tighten his grip on Missy, Barky jumped on the huge raptor, savagely biting him, "Turn her loose or there won't be anything left of you but owl shit!"

The big owl hooted, "What the hell are you doing? I will kill you, too!"

Barky snarled as he continued his assault, "Turn her loose you oversized hummingbird!" Before the owl could react, he was bleeding from numerous bite wounds. "Damn, why does this kind of crap always happen to me? It's just my luck to find the only wolf in a squirrel's body in the entire forest!" The owl realized he was overmatched. He flew away with a mighty flapping of his wings.

Barky barked loudly, "Yeah! And don't come back or my nest will be padded with owl feathers! You don't know who you're messing with!" Barky stalked up and down the limb looking in the direction of the escaping owl, muttering, "I taught that dumb-ass a lesson. He won't be jacking with Ol' Barky anytime soon."

Suddenly he remembered Missy. He turned to her and chattered, "Are you okay?"

Missy was dumbfounded, "How... why... what... how did you do that? Squirrels don't do that."

For one of the few times in his life, Barky thought about what he was going to say. "Well, I guess hanging out with wolves does have some advantages. I've seen them fight. I guess I learned from watching them." He paused for a minute and grinned, "I was pretty terrific, wasn't I?"

Missy could not help but shyly smile. "Actually, you were."

The two squirrels spent the next two days getting to know each other better. As it turned out, Missy was now more than willing to be Barky's mate. They nuzzled and licked each other. The first time Barky rubbed her from behind, Missy demurely raised her tail to accommodate the coupling. When they finished, Barky exclaimed, "Wow!"

Missy drew in her breath sharply and responded, "Double wow!"

They continued to mate many times over the next two days with Missy usually being the aggressor. She would brazenly back up to Barky with her tail raised. Barky never had any objections as he enthusiastically responded to her advances. Barky thought to himself, *"I knew I was good but I didn't know I was this good."*

When they returned to the wolves, Blood Warrior, Tasha and Valor noticed the change in Missy's attitude. They saw the caresses and open affection between the two squirrels. Finally, curiosity got the best of Blood Warrior. "Okay Barky, what happened? When you left here two days ago, Missy couldn't stand to be in the same tree with you. Now, she's all over you!"

Tasha interrupted. "Blood Warrior! That's none of your business!"

Blood Warrior responded, "Maybe it's not but I still want to know how he pulled off this miracle!"

Barky scrunched up his forehead as if he was in deep thought. "The only thing I can tell you is something that would be hard for a wolf is easy for a squirrel."

Missy cut in, "Oh Barky, be nice." She spoke to the wolves, "Barky saved my life when I was attacked by an owl. I've never seen anyone so brave. I thought the owl was going to kill and eat me, but Barky drove him off!" Missy sighed as she dreamily looked at Barky, "I've never met anyone as wonderful as him."

Blood Warrior started to make gagging noises. Tasha gave him a disapproving nip. "Well, I think it's sweet." The wolves and the new squirrel became fast friends.

THINNING
THE PACK

One day while scouting, Blood Warrior cut the tracks of a small pack of four wolves. He stealthily trailed them until he came upon them feeding on a large cow moose they had just killed. They were snarling and snapping greedily at each other even though there was plenty of meat to go around.

#1 growled, "I did the most in killing this moose! I should eat first!"

#7 snapped, "You did not! We wouldn't have even killed this moose if it hadn't been for me!"

#4 snarled, "You two idiots are both crazy! I am the one who killed this moose!"

#10 just snickered as he continued swallowing huge chunks of moose flesh. He thought, *Let them waste time arguing. I will spend my time eating.*

Blood Warrior knew they belonged to Red Fang. He thought, *They will sleep after gorging themselves. That should give me enough time to get Tasha and Valor. Today is the day we whittle down Red Fang's forces a little more. Once I get the odds reduced to an acceptable level, I will openly challenge Red Fang… Red Fang, I'm coming for you.*

Blood Warrior loped up to Tasha and Valor as they were taking an afternoon nap. He barked, "Tasha, Valor—let's go. I have found four of Red Fang's pack. It is time to deal with them."

They followed Blood Warrior at a trot until he slowed to a walk. They crept up to see four wolves soundly sleeping next to a half-eaten moose carcass.

Blood Warrior whispered, "I will take the two who are in the middle. Tasha, you take the one on the far right. Valor, you take the one on the far left." As they slowly stalked into position, Valor accidentally stepped on a branch. The loud snap immediately woke the sleeping wolves.

As Red Fang's wolves growled and bristled, #1 snarled, "Who are you and what do you want?"

Blood Warrior grinned and barked, "If I had any doubts, I don't anymore. Only one of Red Fang's inbreds could be that big of a dumb-ass!" Blood Warrior bared his fangs. "I am the one you have been looking for! Today is judgment day for you and these other three halfwits!"

#1 took a step back in fear at the size of Blood Warrior and muttered to his pack mate standing next to him, "A little help here."

#7 took two steps back, barking, "You're on your own!"

#1 reminded him, "If Red Fang finds out you didn't help me, it will be your ass!"

#7 considered whom he was the most afraid of, Red Fang or this huge wolf in front of him. The fear of Red Fang won out. He decided to fight.

#1 sprang at Blood Warrior, going for his throat and snarling, "No one has ever beaten me in a fight!"

Right behind him, emboldened by #1's attack, #7 leapt at Blood Warrior, screaming, "Die!"

#1 did not make his target. Instead of locking his teeth on the giant wolf's throat, Blood Warrior's quickness resulted in #1's throat being in the vise-like grip of Blood Warrior's jaws. Blood Warrior slung #1's body, using it as a club, to knock down #7 and defeating his attempted assault.

Tasha, using her own superior speed, struck first at #4. She immediately bowled him over and had his throat in a death grip. #4 pleaded, "Noooo! Stop! I never did anything to you!"

Tasha said around a mouthful of his throat, "You helped kill my mate's family! You are going to die for that!"

Valor and #10 were circling each other, looking for a lethal opening. To Valor's dismay, #10 latched on to his leg, breaking the bone. The broken bone caused Valor to go to the ground yipping for help. "Blood Warrior! Tasha!"

#10 gloated, "This was too easy!" But instead of following up on his advantage and finishing off Valor, #10 decided to settle with the defenseless wolf later. He chose to help his pack mates. #10 threw himself at Tasha, knocking her down and causing her to lose her grip on #4. #4 had been close to death, but without Tasha's teeth imbedded in his throat, he had a rush of adrenaline, fueled by the help from his brother and the desperation of being on the verge of death.

Tasha was giving ground under the ferocious onslaught of the two killers. She was bitten severely and blood was streaming from her open wounds. Tasha fought with everything she had but she was losing ground and losing the battle. Valor tried to drag himself on his broken leg to help her but collapsed in defeat. He whimpered miserably as he saw Tasha being killed right before his eyes.

Blood Warrior was still using the lifeless body of #1 to bludgeon #7. He quickly turned his head to check the welfare of Tasha and Valor. What he saw shocked him! Blood Warrior dropped the dead wolf's body, loudly snarling, "Father Wolf!" He jumped and landed between Tasha's attackers. He roared, "Get off her!" as he savagely bit both of the killers. Blood Warrior drove #4 and #10 backward with his furious barrage of fangs and claws.

As they regrouped, they were joined by a recovered #7. The three marauders began circling Blood Warrior, growling and bristling. #10 threatened, "What are you going to now, big wolf? You might beat one of us or maybe even two, but no way you can take all three of us! So, what are you going to do now?"

Blood Warrior calmly stood there without moving a hair on his body, "What am I going to do? I'll tell you what I'm going to do. I'm going to kill you and your two stupid brothers and there is nothing you can do to stop me."

Blood Warrior's muscles began to tense under his thick black fur as he got ready to spring into action and take the fight to them. All three of his adversaries had a bad feeling there was something wrong. They knew they had him outnumbered and the outcome should not be in doubt, but for some reason there was a small knot of doubt in their bellies.

Barky and Missy had followed their friends to this showdown. They had maintained their silence but Barky saw an opportunity to help his friend. He chattered loudly, "Hey, you imbeciles! You're about to get your asses kicked!" While Missy was horrified to hear her mate talk to wolves that way, Blood Warrior knew what Barky was doing. When Barky chattered, the other three wolves distractedly glanced up in the trees. Blood Warrior used Barky's diversion to attack.

Blood Warrior had already calculated who was probably the most dangerous of the three when he singled out #10. #10 was bigger than his brothers. He struck at him first. Blood Warrior's most discernible feature was just the sheer size of him, but what surprised his opponents was his quickness. He was a lightning bolt of death and destruction.

The suddenness of Blood Warrior's attack, coupled with his momentary loss of focus, caused #10 to find himself flat on his back with the big wolf sinking his teeth into his throat. Blood Warrior snarled, "Time to die!"

The other two wolves immediately attacked Blood Warrior. With Tasha and Valor disabled with their wounds, Blood Warrior's life was in peril. #4 closed his jaws on one of Blood Warrior's hamstrings, growling, "You are right! It is time to die, but it will be you and not us!"

#7 bit down on one of Blood Warrior's forelegs in a potentially crippling attack as he added, "You will die, not us!"

Tasha was close to death, but seeing her adored mate losing the battle, she attempted to drag herself to the fight. Her physical strength was at such a low ebb she collapsed again after only a few feet. Tasha whimpered, "Honey, I'm trying." Valor also tried to help Blood Warrior but his broken leg was just too much to overcome.

Blood Warrior knew they were all in dire straits. If he could not kill these renegades, he, Tasha and Valor were going to be dead in a matter of minutes. In the next split second Father Wolf spoke to his mind, *My son, I put you here for a purpose. That purpose is not to die here. I am with you.*

Bolstered by the encouragement from Father Wolf, Blood Warrior felt renewed courage and strength course through his mind and body. He finished #10 with a mighty crunch of his jaws, snapping his neck like it was a twig. Blood Warrior snarled, "Get off me!" as he violently shook his body like he was shaking dry a wet coat. His movement was so fierce that #4 and #7 lost their grip on his body and were sent flying, with each wolf crashing against a tree.

#4 and #7 were instantly back on their feet, but this time their motivation wasn't from an aggressive desire to kill, but one of fear of dying themselves. They were backing up in a defensive posture and furtively glancing around looking for an escape route. Their fear of Red Fang had now been overtaken by their fear of Blood Warrior.

Blood Warrior, battered and bleeding, still advanced toward the wolves. Even with his wounds, he knew that he would not have a better opportunity to reduce Red Fang's odds against him than now. Blood Warrior growled, "I hope you boys aren't planning on leaving anytime soon. The party's just starting."

#4 yipped and sprinted for the nearest thicket. The thick brush presented little problem for Blood Warrior as he bulled his way through it in pursuit of the fleeing wolf. He knocked #4 down and pinned him to the ground with his massive paws. "Where are you going in such a hurry?"

#4 responded, "Red Fang will kill you for this!"

Blood Warrior snarled, "My greatest hope is that he will try." Blood Warrior showed some mercy, by breaking his neck with a swift, powerful bite.

#7 had used Blood Warrior's chase of his brother to try to effect his own escape. Valor was directly in his path as #7 leaped over the fallen wolf. Valor's broken leg rendered him immobile, but otherwise intact. Valor caught the leaping wolf as a bear snags a jumping salmon. He grabbed #7 by the throat and bit down with every ounce of his strength. #7 yelped, "No! Stop! I have to get away!" Valor disregarded his pleas and maintained his grip on #7's throat. #7 snarled, growled and yipped as he thrashed around, violently trying to lessen Valor's death grip.

After dispatching #4, Blood Warrior responded to the din of Valor's struggle to kill #7 by running back to help. He arrived to see the last feeble kicks of #7 as he died. His body lay on top of Valor as Valor had no strength left to shake it off.

THE HEALING

They had killed four more members of Red Fang's pack but at no small cost to themselves. Blood Warrior was wounded and bleeding. Valor had a broken leg which usually carries a death sentence in the animal kingdom. Tasha was near death's door, as evidenced by her slow, shallow breaths.

Tasha was Blood Warrior's immediate concern. He pulled the carcass of #7 off of Valor and dragged it over to where Tasha lay. He positioned the body so when he used his fangs to rip open its belly, the blood flowed down over Tasha's open mouth. As the life-giving blood hit her tongue, she instinctively began to swallow. Blood Warrior bit off tiny chucks of wolf meat and laid them in her mouth to eat. The infusion of the nourishing blood and flesh gave Tasha enough strength to open her eyes. When Blood Warrior saw that her beautiful blue eyes still had life in them, he howled, "Father Wolf, please keep Your promise to me. I cannot do what You want me to do without her. Please save her!"

Tasha continued drinking and eating until she was strong enough to raise her head to apologize. "Honey, I'm sorry I couldn't help you. I tried."

Blood Warrior licked the excess blood from her muzzle as he softly barked, "Tasha, don't be silly. This was my fault for not protecting you better. Now, no more conversation. You need to eat and rest." Tasha laid her head back down and drifted off into a deep sleep.

Blood Warrior turned his attention to Valor. "How are you doing, old friend?" At first Valor grimaced and said, "I'm fine," but Blood Warrior could see the crook in Valor's broken leg. Blood Warrior and Valor looked at each other, neither wanting to acknowledge the obvious. Finally, Valor barked, "I'm as good as dead, aren't I?"

Barky had set a new personal record for not talking, but couldn't stand it any longer. "I want to help. What can I do?"

Missy chimed in, "Me too. I also want to help."

Blood Warrior barked, "I think the way you can help the most is to keep watch so we are not surprised by Red Fang or any more of his bunch."

Barky chattered, "Missy, would you patrol the perimeter and announce any surprise guests?"

Missy crooned, "Of course, my little Flower Blossom!"

As she glided out of sight, Blood Warrior barked to the sheepish Barky, "Flower blossom? Flower blossom? Please tell me she didn't just call you that?"

Barky retorted, "Shut up, wolf! You know nothing!"

Blood Warrior and Barky spent the next hour watching over Tasha and Valor. Blood Warrior was feeling better about Tasha as she was sleeping peacefully and breathing normally. Valor was a different story. He was grunting from the pain in his leg. Finally, Barky said, "I have an idea which, by the way, is normal for squirrels but rare for wolves. If Valor is to have a chance to survive, of course his leg has to heal. But as crooked as it is, even if it heals, he will only be able to hobble and most certainly not be able to run. His only chance at living out his life is to have his leg straightened."

Blood Warrior pondered Barky's idea and barked, "How do we straighten it out?"

Barky snorted, "How the hell should I know! I'm the idea guy. I come up with the good ideas. It's your problem on how to implement them. Use that thick wolf skull of yours to think with once in a while instead of just as a battering ram."

Blood Warrior growled, "I know we're better off having you around, but sometimes it just barely is!"

Blood Warrior approached the suffering Valor. "Super squirrel thinks he may know of a way that you might live."

Valor desperately responded, "What is it? At this point, I'll try anything!"

Blood Warrior said, "Not so fast, because if you think you hurt now, it won't compare to what's ahead. I will have to take your leg in my teeth and forcibly straighten it out."

Valor realized his pain level would multiply significantly as just the slightest touch of his leg sent shock waves of pain through his body. After thinking about it for several minutes, Valor softly barked, "Well, I guess I don't really have much of a choice, do I?"

Blood Warrior shook his head sadly, "No, my friend—not if you want to live."

After steeling his courage, Valor gritted his teeth. "Do what you have to do. As much as I don't want to do this, I even more don't want to die."

Blood Warrior gently took Valor's paw in his mouth and slowly started pulling his leg straight. Valor loudly howled and yipped, but Blood Warrior continued pulling his leg until it was straight.

It was two weeks before the pain had subsided enough for Valor to stand up. It was another two weeks before he could lope on it. Another month passed before he was back to as normal as he was going to get. Valor would always run with a limp, but at least he was now a functional wolf. This episode of dealing with intense pain further strengthened Valor's character. His old life as a coward could no longer be remembered.

Under Blood Warrior's loving care, Tasha was restored to her full strength and vitality. Blood Warrior hunted and kept his pack fed while Barky and Missy watched for intruders.

THE FATHERS

O ne day Missy asked Barky, "Flower Blossom, are you ready for some more little Flower Blossom's?"

Barky paused thoughtfully, "What are you talking about? Wait a minute... Are you saying what I think you're saying?"

Missy chattered excitedly, "Yes silly! What did you think I meant? You are going to be a father!" Barky stood up, then sat down, then stood up, then sat down. Missy interrupted. "Flower Blossom, will you stop that? You're making me nervous!"

Barky started jumping in place. "I'm making you nervous? I'm making *you* nervous! You're making *ME* nervous!"

At the same time on the forest floor, Tasha nuzzled and licked Blood Warrior. "Honey, I have some good news." Blood Warrior said, "What is it? Do you smell a deer? I hope so, because I'm starting to get hungry!"

Tasha sat down and fixed her blue eyes on Blood Warrior's golden eyes, "Nope, it's better than deer meat!" Blood Warrior barked, "Oh come on Tasha, fresh deer meet is your favorite thing. There is nothing better than that to you."

Tasha slyly smiled, "Well, there just might be something better."

Blood Warrior barker louder, "Tasha, you know I don't like playing games. Quit beating around the sumac and tell me plainly!"

Tasha laid her head on his neck and softly said, "You're going to be a father."

It didn't sink in right at first. When the light of recognition came on in Blood Warrior's eyes, he leapt and twisted in the air at the same time, almost knocking down Tasha. *"WHAT?!"*

Tasha laughed. "You are going to be a father!"

Blood Warrior was stunned as he sat down on his haunches. Just then Barky and Missy glided up to the tree over the wolves' heads. Barky and Blood Warrior locked eyes and barked simultaneously, "I'm going to be a father!"

They continued to stare at each other and said in unison again, "What?"

The wolf and the squirrel gaped at each other, dumbfounded, until they shouted yet again, in one voice, "Shut up!"

Tasha interjected, "You boys are fascinating ,but your conversation leaves a little to be desired. Why don't you let the girls see if we can figure out what's going on here?"

Tasha asked Missy, "Are you pregnant?"

Missy giggled, "Yes! Are you?"

Tasha replied, "Yes!" Tasha howled and Missy chattered in excitement.

While this was good news in the wolf and squirrel families, it was also good news to the ears of an unseen intruder. One of Red Fang's killers, #14, had managed to evade the eyes, ears and noses of the wolves and squirrels and had penetrated their surveillance perimeter. She was lying motionless in the shadows as she thought, *I bet Father will welcome me back with a feast in my honor when I tell him about the upcoming wolf and squirrel litters. I know his favorite food is pups of any kind. If he can watch the parents suffer while he eats their offspring, it makes the meat taste even sweeter.*

THE FINAL
HUNT

Red Fang was growing impatient. He had begun regretting his orders of "do not return under penalty of death" if they didn't have proof that Blood Warrior was dead. One night under a full yellow moon, he howled as loudly as he could and waited for answering howls. There were none. Red Fang barked sharply, "Adolph and Brutus, tomorrow at first light, I want you to go and find your idiotic brothers and sisters. Tell them I've changed my mind and I want them to return to me."

Adolph and Brutus gave him a questioning look. Red Fang snarled, "Are you confused? It is a very simple order. Go find your brothers and sisters. Wolf shit! Can you not understand something so simple?"

Brutus stammered, "Well, Fa-Father, will you kill us if we come back without them?"

Red Fang growled, "I will kill you if you don't go and do as I say!"

It took two days for them to find the bodies of #1, #4, #7 and #10. Adolph growled, "I don't get it. Our guys were some pretty tough wolves. What could have killed them?"

Brutus responded, "Can't you see the tracks, dumb-ass? Those are *wolf* tracks!"

#14 had separated from the search party because she had grown weary of her brothers constantly trying to breed her. She had been gone for two days and two nights. The third night #3 barked, "What should we do? I don't think we should leave #14, but how do we find her?"

#8 replied, "Why is it our fault that piece of wolf shit is lost? Let her find us!"

#12 chimed in, "It doesn't make any difference whose fault it is. Father will hold us responsible anyway."

After a few minutes of uneasy silence, #12 threw back his head and loudly howled.

#8 tried to cut him short. "Stop that! Are you nuts? We are telling everybody where we're at! We have no idea where Blood Warrior is. If Father hears your howl and comes to investigate and we don't have any information, we're dead meat!"

#12 barked, "We need to find #14! Have you got any better idea on how we do that? Now, shut up and let's see if #14 answers us back!"

It seemed that #14 was out of earshot of their howls. There was no return howl, just the silence of the night. But that howl was heard as two sets of ears pricked up. Adolph and Brutus set out in the direction of the howl. Adolph and

Brutus slipped quietly through the dark forest. When they got within sight of their pack mates, they stood in the shadows and watched them.

#8 snarled softly to himself, "Damn you, #14. We have a job to do and it doesn't include searching for your dumb-ass." Brutus spoke from the darkness, startling the three wolves. "And just what is this job you are supposed to be doing?"

Adolph and Brutus stepped out of the shadows, causing their three brothers to frantically search with their eyes to see if Red Fang was with them. Adolph barked, "Relax, Father is not with us. In fact, he has changed his mind and sent us to fetch you back."

Brutus asked, "Just how long has #14 been gone?"

#8 snapped, "The stupid bitch has been gone for two days. I say we leave her. She wasn't much help anyway. If we couldn't breed her, she would have been totally worthless."

Just then, a crunch in the leaves caused all five wolves to whirl, growling with bared fangs. #14 walked up to them with a pleased look on her face. "Worthless, huh? I've done something you bunch of fools haven't done! I've found Blood Warrior!"

Adolph commanded, "We need to take that information to Father right away!" All six wolves began their trip back to Red Fang, single file, with Adolph in the lead.

It took two days for them to get back to Red Fang and Delilah. Red Fang greeted them, "I assume you have some good news for me?"

Brutus started to speak but #14 cut him off. "Shut up, Brutus! This is my good news so don't try to take the credit for it! You and the rest of my worthless brothers haven't done anything except eat, sleep and shit." Turning to Red Fang, she barked excitedly, "Father, I have found Blood Warrior! And that's not all. His bitch is pregnant. Also, that damn Barky has found a mate and his bitch is also pregnant. Father, are you proud of me?"

Red Fang approached #14 and began licking her face and muzzle. The rest of the wolves were astonished at his show of affection. None could recall that ever happening before. Delilah was the most affected as she was deeply jealous. Red Fang had never been affectionate with her. At that moment Delilah started scheming how she could kill her daughter.

Red Fang barked to #14, "It's a shame you weren't born with a penis and testicles. You would have made a much better son than these pinheads who are supposed to be my sons!" His five sons looked at the ground, avoiding eye contact with their father. They hated what he said but were too fearful of him for a confrontation. They, too, would now like to see their sister dead.

Red Fang announced, "#14, you will no longer be known by a number. Your new name is Delilah. Old Delilah, you will now be called #14. The new Delilah is taking your place." The old Delilah staggered backward in shock but she did not challenge Red Fang's decision. She knew that any challenge would result in her death.

The new Delilah was proud of her new name. Red Fang's sons were not the least bit upset at the loss of position of their mother because they simply did not care about any members of the pack except themselves. Red Fang left at dawn with his pack to find Blood Warrior with the new Delilah serving as his guide.

One morning Blood Warrior, Tasha and Valor were resting after killing and devouring a cow elk the previous night. Tasha and Valor had no problem dozing, but every time Blood Warrior closed his eyes, they popped back open. Finally, he got on his feet and began to pace back and forth.

Tasha woke and softly barked, "What's the matter, honey? Why can't you sleep?"

Blood Warrior stretched and yawned. "I don't know why. I'm sleepy, but I can't relax enough to get to sleep. Every time I try, I feel a sense of danger and the hair stands up on the back of my neck."

Tasha asked, "What do you think it is?"

Blood Warrior thought and replied, "I don't know. That's the frustrating part. I just sense there is something evil headed our way."

Blood Warrior looked up in the trees and saw Barky and Missy petting and licking each other. Blood Warrior said, "Barky, if you can quit being Flower Blossom for a few minutes, I need you to help me check out our surroundings."

Despite Blood Warrior's sarcasm, Barky could see from the look on his face that Blood Warrior was serious, "Okay my friend, are we looking for anyone or anything in particular?"

Blood Warrior furrowed his brow. "I don't really know just exactly what it is. I sense it more than anything else."

Barky responded, "I've never known your senses to be wrong. Let's go in opposite directions and see if we can find the source of your discomfort."

Tasha and Valor were no longer napping but were on full alert. Blood Warrior barked, "Tasha, I need you and Valor to stay here until we have done a search around our location."

Tasha said, "We should help."

Valor seconded, "Yes, we can provide more eyes to look."

Blood Warrior shook his head. "No, I don't want us to get separated. Just stay here, but be ready to go at a moment's notice!"

Barky told Missy, "I want you to stay in the den until we get back." Missy gave him a quick lick. "Be careful, my Flower Blossom."

Barky had covered several miles when he saw the source of Blood Warrior's premonition: eight wolves. They had stopped and were softly barking. Barky flattened himself against a tree trunk when he heard Red Fang say, "Delilah, are you sure we are headed in the right direction?"

The new Delilah looked around to double-check her bearings. "Yes, Father, I am sure we are headed to where I saw Blood Warrior and his friends." Red Fang resumed the journey in the direction indicated by the new Delilah.

Barky was careful to keep a large tree between him and the renegade wolf pack to hide his flight as he sailed back to the den.

When Barky got back to the den area, Blood Warrior had already returned from his reconnaissance. Barky sharply chattered, "It's Red Fang and he's got seven more wolves with him!"

Blood Warrior responded, "How much time do we have?"

Barky said, "They are going slowly and carefully, trying to catch us unawares. We have a little time before they get here, but not a lot."

Blood Warrior looked at Tasha and Valor. "I want you two to leave our home territory and don't come back until I come get you!"

Tasha protested, "*NO!* I'm not leaving you here to fight those monsters by yourself!"

Valor chimed in, "Me either, my brother. I will not leave your side!"

Blood Warrior was firm. "Tasha, you are carrying our children in your belly. I need to know that you and they are safe! Valor, I would love to have you fight beside me but I need you to protect our family. Will you do that for me?"

Valor bristled at the thought of the family being threatened. "Of course, my brother! I would do anything for you!"

Tasha hesitated with tears in her eyes. "The safety of our children is the only reason that I would ever leave you."

Blood Warrior commanded, "Go! Go now! I will lead Red Fang away from you!" Tasha and Valor loped off in the direction indicated by Blood Warrior.

Blood Warrior saw Barky and Missy in a nearby pine tree. "Barky, I know you and Missy are probably safe in the trees, but I want to be completely sure that you and your family are all right. Take her and follow Tasha and Valor away from here!"

Barky paused, looking back and forth between Missy and Blood Warrior. Blood Warrior interjected, "Go, my friend! Protect your family! The best thing you can do for me is to help me know that your family is secure. Go, quickly!"

Barky said, "May Father Squirrel bless you and keep you safe! I will see you again!" Barky and Missy glided off, tracking the direction of Tasha and Valor.

Blood Warrior turned to face the evil threat. He fearlessly jogged off to meet Red Fang and his pack. Blood Warrior spotted the vile wolves before they saw him. He carefully hid himself in the total darkness of the dense sumac.

Red Fang and his gang were slowly creeping through the forest when they were startled by the sudden howl of a wolf. Sudden fear wrenched the bodies of each of the wolves. What made it even more unnerving was that the howl was close by. They couldn't tell where the howl originated as the sound was diffused due to the thick brush, but it felt like the howler was standing next to them.

Blood Warrior laughed from somewhere in the darkness. "What's the matter, Red Fang? Are you afraid of me? One wolf against eight. Surely the eight of you can handle a lone wolf!"

All of the pack bristled as Red Fang snarled, "Show yourself, Blood Warrior, and we shall see who is afraid! Or are you like your craven father who cried like a pup begging for his life when we killed him?"

Blood Warrior growled, "I know my father well enough to know that didn't happen! Plus, I had an eye witness who told me how bravely Thunder fought! So save your lies for those stupid enough to believe them, like this bunch of halfwits who are dumb enough to follow you!"

Red Fang was enraged. "What you are saying is total wolf shit! You are all bark and no bite! Come out and fight me! It will just be you and me! The others won't interfere!" Red Fang waited to see if Blood Warrior was going to believe his lie.

Blood Warrior laughed again from the blackness, "You think you are smarter than everyone else! Your problem is you are judging yourself against the company you keep."

Blood Warrior snarled loudly, addressing all the wolves, "I have killed a wolverine, an eagle and a cougar! I have even killed the largest grizzly bear in the forest! I have also killed four of your pack members! What makes you fools think you can kill me? Red Fang is leading you to a sure death! The best thing you can do is turn around and take your asses away from here! In fact, you need to leave this entire territory before I lose what's left of my patience and kill all of you!"

All the wolves except Red Fang began to cast furtive glances, fearfully looking for Blood Warrior. Suddenly, Adolph excitedly barked, "Here he is! I smell him in this sumac thicket!" Red Fang snarled loudly, "Don't just stand there, you idiots! Get him!" All seven members of his pack dove into the thicket.

THE DARK
BATTLE

Red Fang could not see what was going on due to the dense brush, but he heard the sound of a fearsome fight. The birds and animals in the area cautiously approached. They had never heard such a din of loud growls, snarls, yips and howls. Their curiosity compelled them to find the source of this awful racket, but they stayed poised to flee at the first sign of danger to themselves.

Brutus and Adolph were the first to reach Blood Warrior. Their attack was ferocious and furious. Fighting in the thicket was a calculated risk on Blood Warrior's part. He knew he stood little chance of fighting against eight wolves in open ground. Blood Warrior used the brush as a line of defense. All the wolves could not reach him at the same time.

Blood Warrior met Adolph's assault head on, both fiercely grappling for each other's throat. Blood Warrior's sheer strength overpowered Adolph. Blood Warrior's jaws closed around Adolph's throat in a death grip. Brutus had flanked Blood Warrior and had a clear shot at an exposed hamstring. Brutus delayed biting his hamstring, thinking, *I will give Blood*

Warrior a few more seconds to finish killing my brother. With him dead, I will have to be Father's favorite.

As soon as Brutus saw Adolph's body go limp, he locked his strong jaws on Blood Warrior's hamstring. At that point #3 and #8 broke through the brush and set on the besieged Blood Warrior, one going for his throat and the other the back of his neck.

Blood Warrior knew he was close to being killed. If the present circumstances weren't altered drastically in the next few seconds, he would be dead. In a split second, pictures of his father, mother, brothers, sisters, Barky, Missy, Valor and most importantly, Tasha, flashed through his mind. With a roar that sounded more like a grizzly bear than a wolf, Blood Warrior swung his head, knocking down #3 and #8. He knew he had to do something before Brutus sliced through his hamstring, crippling him and condemning him to death.

With Brutus gnawing on his hamstring, Blood Warrior stretched for the only thing he could reach: an ear. Blood Warrior snapped his powerful jaws shut on the ear and pulled with all his strength. Brutus's ear came off in Blood Warrior's mouth. Brutus could not contain a yelp of pain, loosening his hold on Blood Warrior's leg. When Blood Warrior felt the pressure lessen, he snatched his leg from Brutus's jaws.

#3 and #8 hesitated renewing their attack. Fear had actually motivated their previous attack and that exact same fear began to paralyze them. They watched in horror as Blood Warrior made short work of Brutus, splintering his spine with one crunch of his potent fangs.

Brutus wiggled as his lower limbs no longer worked, mewing like a puppy, "Please, please, please, don't kill me! I don't want to die!"

Blood Warrior growled, "Funny, you weren't too concerned about me dying a minute ago!" Seeing Brutus was no longer a threat, Blood Warrior quickly turned to assess more of his opponents.

He saw that #3 and #8 and been joined by #12. They weren't advancing but were in more of a defensive posture. The close quarters of the thicket would not allow them to spread out. Blood Warrior briefly thought about letting them go free but concluded that doing so would not serve justice nor Father Wolf. The only fair judgment for their acts was death. Mercy is rarely shown in the animal kingdom.

#12 whined, "Let us go, Blood Warrior. We promise to leave the territory and never come back!"

Blood Warrior snarled, "You made your decisions that led you to this point and I have made mine. Father Wolf has sentenced you to death and has chosen me as the executioner."

#3 blasphemed, "To hell with Father Wolf and to hell with you! Do you think I can't see that you have already lost a lot of blood? We can finish you and we will do it now!" #3 sprang at Blood Warrior's throat with bared fangs. In the next instant #8 and #12 joined their brother in their desperate attack. They gambled everything on this brutal blitz.

In his weakened condition, Blood Warrior went down on his back from the savage onslaught. All three attackers were frantically biting and scratching him. #3 snarled, "This is the end for you! Prepare to meet this Father Wolf you claim to know!"

Blood Warrior was returning every bite with a bite and every scratch with a scratch despite being outnumbered, but his strength was rapidly bleeding from his body. Just as he was about to slip into unconsciousness, Father Wolf appeared in his mind. *Take courage, my son. I did not bring you this far to abandon you. I am with you!*

A renewed strength flowed through Blood Warrior's body. The three assailants were shocked when Blood Warrior bounded to his feet, shaking all three of them off. #3's last words were, "What the hell?" as Blood Warrior tore his throat out. #8 and #12 were frozen with fear, allowing Blood Warrior to fracture each of their necks with a strong snap of his jaws. They never resisted, but meekly stood there and accepted their fate. Blood Warrior did show some mercy to Brutus as he quickly ended his suffering and his life with a quick chomp on the back of his neck.

Blood Warrior collapsed in exhaustion and from a lack of blood. If Red Fang had known this, he could have leisurely strolled into the ticket and easily killed Blood Warrior. But, Red Fang did not know Blood Warrior's condition because he was too big of a coward to go into the sumac. His cravenness cost him his chance to be the victor in this epic battle.

When the battle raged at its fiercest amidst the tremendous noise, confusion and chaos, the old Delilah stood slightly behind the new Delilah as both wolves crept forward, apprehensively looking for an opening that would allow them to join the fight. The old Delilah could care less about killing Blood Warrior, but there was a wolf whom she desperately wanted to kill.

With the new Delilah totally focused on finding a way through the thicket to the fight, her mother saw the perfect opening and latched onto her daughter's neck. The new Delilah shrilly yipped, "Mother! What are you doing? Why are you doing this?"

The new Delilah violently twisted and turned, attempting to dislodge her mother from her back. The old Delilah responded to her daughter's pleas by tightening her jaws. Finally, her neck cracked and the new Delilah fell dead.

The old Delilah softly growled, "You ungrateful bitch! I gave birth to you and you thought you were going to replace me? I don't think so." The old Delilah slunk from the thicket and saw the anxious Red Fang trying to peer into the thicket to see what was happening.

The old Delilah ran up to him and loudly barked, "Red Fang, it was horrible! Blood Warrior has killed them all, all five boys and Delilah! I think he is a demon! Let's get away from here before he comes after us and kills us too!"

Red Fang looked back and forth between the old Delilah and the thicket several times before saying, "You may be right. Maybe we should go."

The old Delilah enthusiastically responded, "Yes, we can start over! Just you and me, just like the old days! We can start a new pack! It will be bigger and better than the old one!"

Red Fang barked, "It doesn't look like we have any choice, #14!"

The old Delilah gently barked as she nuzzled Red Fang, "Can I go back to my old name of Delilah?"

Red Fang thought for a moment before agreeing, "What the hell. I guess it doesn't make any difference now. I will call you Delilah again."

FINDING TASHA

Blood Warrior lay at death's door. He drifted in and out of consciousness. He knew he was hurt badly, but for some reason he never felt like he was going to die. He did know that he had to have some sleep. While he slept, his body slowly began healing itself.

After three days, Blood Warrior shakily rose to his feet. He knew he had to eat and soon. In three days, he had lost almost 50 pounds as his body burned his stored fat and finally started on his muscle mass in the healing process.

With the remembrance of Father Wolf's encouragement, Blood Warrior felt his body being reenergized. After a short hunt, he caught a whiff of the scent of a deer. Following the scent, he soon spotted a small doe grazing in a little grove of trees. It was a perfect setup, with ample cover concealing him until he got within range.

Blood Warrior charged the deer. He was on her before she saw or smelled him. Death was instantaneous. As Blood Warrior fed, his body and spirit were renewed with the life-giving flesh and blood. He ate the entire deer all at once and lay down for a contented sleep.

Red Fang decided to leave his home territory until he could reorganize and determine a course of action. He definitely did not want to tangle with Blood Warrior again until he had a winning plan. He realized he had underestimated Blood Warrior. Red Fang vowed to himself, *I will never have another battle plan that doesn't account for all possible outcomes.*

There was a change of his immediate plans when he cut a pair of wolf tracks leading out of the territory. Red Fang sniffed the spoor, "Ahh, I recognize the smell of Tasha. The second set of tracks must be the third member of their pack. They are too small to be Blood Warrior's." Red Fang immediately visualized what the delicious mating of him and Tasha would be like. Delilah couldn't help but notice his body's obvious reaction to his daydream.

Delilah nuzzled and licked him to take his mind off Tasha. "Red Fang, shouldn't we just ignore them and go make a new home? I want to get started having more litters to restock our pack."

Red Fang snarled, "Shut up! I will do all the thinking for the both of us!" After a short period of silence, he barked, "We are going to follow them and see where they go. Although there is one thing that does bother me. Why isn't Blood Warrior with them? Are you sure he was in good health at the end of the fight?"

Delilah lied, "Yes, he was standing over the bodies of our children. He laughed as he started eating them."

Red Fang growled, "That son of a bitch will pay for that!" He was not upset at the deaths of his children. Red Fang was livid over being beaten by Blood Warrior. He did not know that it would be almost a week before Blood Warrior would be strong enough to trail Tasha and Valor.

Tasha and Valor did not try to hide their tracks. The wanted to make sure that Blood Warrior would find them. Barky and Missy caught up with them and joined their journey. Tasha barked to Valor and the two squirrels, "I wonder how far Blood Warrior wants us to go?"

Barky chattered, "I think we should travel for two days. That should be far enough to keep you and Missy safe from Red Fang."

Valor wished out loud, "I hope Blood Warrior is going to be all right!"

Tasha responded, "Shush, Valor! I don't want to hear that kind of talk! Of course he's going to be all right! I am not going to consider anything but that!"

Valor quickly replied, "Of course he is, Tasha! I didn't mean anything by that."

Barky added, "The big wolf will definitely be okay! Nothing can hurt him!"

Missy chimed in, "Absolutely, Blood Warrior will be fine. I expect to see him at any minute!"

Tasha turned away so they couldn't see the tears in her eyes and whispered to herself, "Please Honey, come back to me. Life is not worth living without you."

From the shadows of a thicket, Red Fang spotted the two wolves across a wide meadow. He and Delilah followed them until they laid down for the night. Red Fang whispered in

Delilah's ear, "Stay here." Silently, Red Fang crept within hearing distance.

Missy chattered to Tasha, "How are you doing, dear? Are the little ones in your belly well?"

Tasha barked cheerfully, "I am fine and my babies seem to be doing well, too. How about you and your children? Is all well?"

Missy responded, "My children are becoming more active in my belly. I am so looking forward to us raising our children together! I can't wait!" Tasha replied, "Me either! It is going to be so much fun!"

Barky said, "I think this is a good place to wait on Blood Warrior. We are far enough away from Red Fang that he should not be a problem to us." Red Fang lay under the cover of darkness and thought, *That's what you think, squirrel,* as he inched away from the wolves and squirrels and skulked back to Delilah.

HAWK'S HELPER

As the sun peaked over the horizon announcing the coming day, Red Fang saw a red-tailed hawk in the top of a tree carefully surveying the sky and the earth for his next meal. Red Fang barked up at the hawk, "Hey hawk, I can tell you where to find a fat squirrel!"

The hawk looked suspiciously at the wolf. "And, why would you do that?"

Red Fang shrugged. "I hate squirrels, but I can't climb trees or fly to kill them!" The hawk cocked his head from side to side, observing Red Fang and trying to figure out the real reason a wolf would want to help a hawk.

Red Fang growled loudly, "See that largest lodgepole pine on that far ridge? There are actually two squirrels in that tree. One is plump and should make you a tasty meal."

The hawk shrieked, "Father Hawk, I never thought I would see the day that a damn wolf would help me hunt."

The hawk climbed high in the cloudless blue sky until he was just a dot. As he sailed, he scanned the tree looking for the squirrels. Spotting his prey, he folded his wings to dive to his target.

Unaware of the approaching killer, Barky said to Missy, "How are you feeling today? Can I get you anything?"

Missy lovingly responded, "No, my little Flower Blossom. I am fi..." Missy was interrupted as she was plucked off the limb by the hawk. Barky's shock at his beloved Missy being snatched from mere inches away was replaced by a killing rage. Barky shot off the limb, spreading his skin as thin as he could get it to get maximum lift in the air.

Missy screamed as the hawk nonchalantly turned his dive around and started to climb, "BARKY!!!"

The hawk had his wiggling catch secure in his talons. He knew nothing could stop him now from enjoying eating the fat squirrel. Suddenly the hawk was knocked sideways in the air as Barky struck him with the full force of his glide. Barky began savagely biting and scratching the hawk. The added weight of Barky's body to the squirming Missy slowly forced the befuddled hawk to the ground.

Tasha and Valor had watched the hawk's attack on Missy in horror. Tasha prayed, "Father Wolf, help them!" As the hawk and the two squirrels approached the ground, Valor readied himself to join in the fight. When the hawk was a few feet from the ground, Valor jumped, grabbing the raptor by his head. Upon hitting the ground, the forceful jaws of the wolf chopped off the hawk's head. For good measure, Valor swallowed the head in one gulp.

The hawk's dying spasm caused him to release Missy from his claws. Her body was limp and her eyes were closed. Barky and Tasha immediately began licking her. Barky begged, "Please Father Squirrel, let her be all right!"

Tasha barked excitedly, "Missy! Missy! Are you okay?"

Missy opened her eyes and gingerly began to move around. "I think... I think I'm fine. Nothing seems to be broken. I'm just scared more than anything else."

Barky chattered loudly, "You are scared? You are scared? I could have crapped a pinecone!"

Missy licked and nuzzled him as she replied, "I shouldn't have been scared. I should have known you would rescue me."

Barky was still trembling from fear and rage. He looked at Valor. "Thank you, my friend! I only hope that someday I can return the favor."

Valor dug his paw in the dirt. "I didn't do much, but I am glad I could help."

Tasha beamed, "We have a team of heroes: squirrels and wolves."

Red Fang and Delilah had watched the failed attempt of the hawk from the shadows on a far ridge that was out of the hearing of those he had targeted for death. Red Fang snarled disgustedly, "You've got to be shitting me! How in the hell can a hawk not kill a squirrel? I'm cursed! I'm surrounded by dumb-asses!" He stalked around in circles, considering taking out his frustrations out on Delilah. Delilah was terrified as she had seen that look in Red Fang's eyes before. When he was in that foul a mood, it usually ended with someone dying.

Red Fang briefly considered killing her, but in the end decided that he needed her to produce more pups to repopulate his pack. Red Fang whined, "Father Wolf, what have I ever done to you? Why are you treating me this way? I don't get it!"

Delilah thought to herself, *Seriously, you don't know why Father Wolf doesn't favor you? I can think of ten reasons right off the top of my head.*

Red Fang and Delilah watched the wolves and squirrels for the next two days, looking for a chance to kill them without taking too big a risk themselves.

Tasha and Valor killed an elk and satisfied their appetites. They had enough meat to last for several days without doing anything but lay around and eat. Valor teasingly barked at Barky, "My friend, we will share our meat with you. Do you want some?"

Barky frowned. "Do you want me to puke on you? That's what would happen if I tried to eat that disgusting bloody meat! I'll stick with my delicious nuts."

A deep voice growled from behind a large aspen, "Is this what happens when I leave you unsupervised?" The surprised Tasha and Valor jumped to their feet bristling and growling. Barky and Missy tensed up, not knowing what to expect.

Blood Warrior laughingly stepped out from behind the tree into the sunshine. Tasha shrieked, "Honey!" as she bounded over to him, almost knocking him down in her exuberance. She licked him from head to toe as her tail wagged furiously. Valor gave her a little time before he joined the lick-fest, "My brother, it is so good to see you!"

Barky and Missy joyously hopped up and down on a limb. Barky chattered, "It's about time! I thought I was going to have to go back and kick Red Fang's ass to bail you out!"

Blood Warrior laughed, "There was a time there when I could have used you!"

Missy barked, "Welcome back!"

When everyone's emotions calmed down, Barky asked, "Did you kill that damn Red Fang?"

Blood Warrior sighed, "Unfortunately, no." He went on to describe the fight and how it took him a number of days to recover from his wounds. Blood Warrior summed it up, "I ended up killing five males of his pack, but there was something that didn't make sense. There was a sixth dead wolf, a female. I didn't kill her and I don't know who did. But regardless of that, I think that we've pretty much wiped out his pack. As far as I know, Red Fang and his bitch are the only ones left alive."

Valor proudly said, "I guess we are safe now from Red Fang. We have destroyed his pack!"

Blood Warrior thought about it and finally said, "Valor, you would be right if it was any sane wolf, but I don't know about Red Fang. He's as crazy as a rabid skunk. I just have this uneasy feeling we may not have seen the last of him."

RED FANG
INVADES

Having observed the reunion of Blood Warrior with his pack from a considerable distance, Red Fang muttered, "Damn him. I will kill him if it's the last thing I do."

Red Fang knew that he had to have reinforcements. It would have been suicidal for him and Delilah to try to go up against Blood Warrior and his two wolves.

Red Fang growled at Delilah to follow him as he set out to put a great distance between them and Blood Warrior. As he traveled, a plan began to take shape in his mind. Two nights later, Red Fang heard the howl of a distant wolf. He barked sharply to Delilah, "Let's go! I hear the sound of our new pack!" Delilah was confused but knew better than to question him.

The cloudless night sky was lit by the shining of the stars and a half moon. By the time Red Fang and Delilah reached the wolf pack, all the wolves were howling at one time. Red Fang answered their howls with one of his own at a short 100 feet away. The startled wolves abruptly stopped their howling.

Red Fang trotted up to them barking, "Well, hello my friends! It's a fine night to be a wolf, isn't it?" The alpha male stepped forward snarling, "We are not your friends! You need to leave our territory! Didn't you smell our scent markers?"

There were five other wolves behind the alpha male, all growling and bristling. To take control of the pack, Red Fang knew he had to kill their leader and he had to do it quickly before he would be overwhelmed by the others. Red Fang slinked up next to the leader, maintaining a submissive posture and whined, "Ease up, my friend. I don't mean you any harm."

The alpha relaxed a bit and replied, "You are still not welcome here. You need to lea…" Red Fang cut him off with a vicious lunge at the leader's throat, ripping it out in a matter of seconds. As the dead alpha collapsed to the ground, the rest of the wolves were frozen in shock.

Red Fang puffed himself up to his maximum size as he snarled, "I am your new leader! My name is Red Fang! You will do as I command!"

The rest of the wolves exchanged glances before their collective body language acknowledged his authority. The law of the pack demanded they follow their leader. Another law allowed a pack leader to be replaced if he was bested in a fight by a wolf who desired to be the leader.

As a further show of dominance, Red Fang singled out the alpha female, mounted and bred her in front of his new pack. The female submitted to her new leader. Over the next two weeks, Red Fang reinforced his leadership by correcting and disciplining the pack members to quickly obey his orders. Most of the wolves had wounds from his painful bites. There were three females including the alpha female. Counting Delilah, this swelled his harem to four females. Red Fang bred each of them repeatedly.

Red Fang thought to himself and smiled, *This is a good start. It damn sure beats waiting for a litter to grow up before they're of any use to me. I should have thought of this a long time ago. Taking over other packs by killing their leader is a genius way to build my pack. When I add one more pack, I will take the whole bunch and seek out Blood Warrior. His days are numbered.*

NEW FAMILIES

T asha began digging in the earth. Blood Warrior questioned her, "Tasha, what are you doing?"

Tasha stopped digging long enough to say, "Honey, it's time."

Blood Warrior was bewildered, "Time for what?" Tasha stopped again and gave him an exasperated look, "Time for you to be a father."

Blood Warrior loudly barked, "WHAT?" He sat back on his haunches, stunned. Tasha kept digging.

Meanwhile Barky chattered to Missy, who was still in their den in the hollow of the tree, "Look, Missy. Tasha is digging a hole. I wonder why she is doing that."

Missy responded, "Probably for the same reason that I've stayed in our den today."

Barky hadn't given it much thought but now he was curious, "Well, why *are* you still in the den?"

Missy replied, "Because my little Flower Blossom, you are about to become a father."

Barky loudly barked, "WHAT?" He sat back on his haunches, stunned. Missy giggled.

When they recovered from their shock, Blood Warrior and Barky looked at each other and shouted in unison, "I'M GOING TO BE A FATHER!"

Barky immediately chattered, "Not this same shit again! Just shut up and let me talk!"

Blood Warrior retorted, "If I shut up every time you wanted to talk, I would never get to say anything!"

Tasha gave birth to five males and one female. All six pups were black with golden eyes. They named the five males Thunder, Zev, Digger, Ulrich and Raul in honor of Blood Warrior's father and brothers. He had asked Tasha, "Do you want to name any of the pups after your family members?"

Tasha barked," Not yet. Let's name this litter after your family. We will name the next litter after my family. Our daughter should be called Shadow after your brave mother." Blood Warrior's response was to lick Tasha's muzzle in appreciation.

Missy gave birth to two males and two females. The males looked like Barky and the females looked like her. Missy chattered, "Have you given any consideration to naming our children?"

Barky responded, "Actually, I have. I think the boys should be called Barky 1 and Barky 2. The girls should be named Barkette 1 and Barkette 2."

Missy laughed, "No, seriously. What should we name them?"

Barky replied, "I am serious! Those are great names!"

Missy then also got serious, "We are NOT naming them that, Bucky!" Whenever Missy was really mad at Barky, she reverted to calling him Bucky.

Barky chattered loudly, "Okay! Okay! You don't have to be so touchy! And for the hundredth time, don't call me Bucky!"

The next day Barky said, "All right, what about this? Let's call the boys Warrior and Valor, and name the girls Little Missy and Tasha."

Missy snuggled up to Barky. "I think those names are wonderful. And I think it's very unselfish of you not to name one of the boys after you."

Barky said, "What are you talking about? One of the boys is named after me!"

Missy was confused. "I don't understand."

Barky retorted, "Warrior is named after me! Who else would you think of if some said the name Warrior?" Missy just giggled.

This was the most joyful and peaceful of times in the lives of the wolves and the squirrels.

Valor became Uncle Valor to both the wolf and the squirrel pups. The squirrel pup named after him swelled up in pride whenever he saw his namesake. The squirrel pups took great delight in watching the wolf pups romp and pummel each other. The squirrels knew they were too small to play with the wolf pups. Instead, they pretended to be "tree wolves" by stalking and pouncing on each other as they mimicked their wolf counterparts.

Red Fang's new pack became a proficient hunting machine. They had to admit that Red Fang knew how to lead the pack to find food, but all of them, deep down, missed their old pack leader and resented the tyrannical rule of Red Fang. Red Fang would not even let them use their old names. He just referred to each of them as "Hey You."

Red Fang took his new pack and began to roam the countryside. None of the other wolves knew what was going on, but they knew not to ask. After a late night howling session, Red Fang detected a faint answering howl far to the south.

At daylight, Red Fang marshaled his troops and struck out in search of the other pack. It was relatively easy to find their tracks. Red Fang trailed them with his pack members in single file behind him. When they caught up with the other pack, Red Fang saw there were five wolves in their pack.

Red Fang approached them in a nonthreatening manner, softly barking, "Hello, friends! Isn't it a great day?" A number of Red Fang's new pack members cringed as they recalled him feigning friendship to get close enough to kill their old leader.

The alpha male moved to the front of his pack. "How can we help you, friend?"

Red Fang moved closer. "As you can see, we're out of our territory and I'm terribly sorry for trespassing on yours, but we had some passing wolves tell us about a large elk herd that was supposed to be in this area. Can you tell us where they might be?"

The alpha wolf was puzzled but turned his head to ask his pack, "Did any of you see..." Red Fang interrupted him by using this advantage to rip the wolf's throat from his body with his razor sharp teeth. What happened next was a virtual repeat of his takeover of the first pack, complete with breeding the alpha female.

Counting Delilah, Red Fang now had ten followers. He waited another month to make sure all of his new pack members were well versed in taking orders and executing them instantly.

THE BETRAYAL

One morning Red Fang decided it was time to start back to the last place he saw Blood Warrior. His pack dutifully, if unenthusiastically, followed him. He was confident that he had the perfect plan of attack. He was looking forward to licking the blood from Blood Warrior's lifeless body and adding Tasha to his harem.

When they got close to the targeted area, Red Fang didn't trust any of the other wolves with the reconnaissance. He did the scouting himself. He left Delilah in charge of the pack. Normally, that authority would fall to another male, but Delilah was the only one who he knew for a fact would not betray him if given the chance. She had also proven to the other wolves that she was Red Fang's equal when it came to being ruthless and vicious. Whenever Red Fang was not around, Delilah assumed his roll of disciplinarian, biting and scratching the subordinate wolves for any perceived infractions to her orders, no matter how minor. The other wolves came to prefer being under the villainous Red Fang's watchful eye than being subjected to Delilah's depravity.

Red Fang caught a glimpse of a wolf off in the distance. Knowing he was close, he immediately hid until he was cloaked by the dark night. He cautiously and silently inched forward until he had a clear view of Blood Warrior, Tasha, Valor and the young pups. He also noticed Barky, Missy and their pups high in the trees. Red Fang grinned as he thought, *This is going to be sweeter than the taste of honey. I will keep Blood Warrior alive long enough so he can see me kill and eat his pups.* It took all of Red Fang's willpower to keep himself from laughing out loud.

When Red Fang got back to his pack he gave each wolf a step-by-step instruction regarding their role in the planned attack at dawn. He made each one repeat his order back to him. This time there would be no slip-ups. At first light, Red Fang dispersed his pack members to their appointed positions. They began to close their noose around the victims.

Blood Warrior smelled them at the same time Barky saw them. Barky loudly chattered the alert, "Danger! Danger! Danger!"

Blood Warrior gathered his wolves into a tight circle of his own. Blood Warrior growled, "Tasha, Valor, put the children in the middle!"

Red Fang strutted out to show himself to Blood Warrior. "Well, well, well, old friend. This day has been a long time coming, but it's here now." Red Fang smirked. "Take a good look at your spawn. It will be the last time you will ever see them and it will be the last time they will ever see you!"

Blood Warrior snarled, "You are not going to know what happens because you will be the first one to die!"

Red Fang laughed. "Really? I don't think so. I'm not stupid. In fact, this time, I've thought of everything! My wolves are under orders to kill your pups if you leave them to come after me!"

Worry began to creep into Blood Warrior's mind. *How can I protect my family from these other wolves and kill Red Fang at the same time?*

It was a standoff as each side hesitated to attack the other side. The stalemate was broken in a completely unpredictable and shocking way. The alpha female from the first pack that Red Fang had taken over barked, "I can't take any more of this! I will not be a part of killing babies! I would rather die first!" She walked over to Tasha, "Can I fight by your side, sister?"

Looking into her eyes, Tasha sensed she was sincere and it was not some trick planned by Red Fang. Tasha moved over to make room for her, "Welcome to the family."

The alpha female from the second pack also approached Tasha. "Have you got room for me, sister? I will fight for your babies!" Tasha moved yet again, allowing the second female to back up to the pups as she bared her teeth prepared to fight to the death.

The defections of two of his wolves infuriated Red Fang. He roared to the rest of his pack, "KILL THEM! KILL THEM ALL!" Red Fang expected a flurry of action, but he was amazed when no one moved. One of the male wolves snarled at Red Fang, "I think I can speak for us all, except for that murderous bitch you call a mate, when I say that we're tired of your shit! We will no longer follow you or take your orders! You might kill us or we might kill you, but either way, we're done with you!"

Showing they were in agreement, the rest of the wolves except for Delilah backed away and sat down.

Barky was jumping up and down, screaming, "How do you like them pine nuts, Red Fang? We'll see how big you are when you have to face Blood Warrior wolf to wolf! DUMB-ASS!"

Behind Barky, the little squirrel pup named Warrior squeaked, "Dumb-ass!"

Missy shot Barky a look of "see what you're teaching our children." Barky sidled over to his son and whispered in his ear to Missy's horror, "That's my boy!"

THE FINAL
REVENGE

The only two marauders left to fight Blood Warrior were Red Fang and Delilah. Tasha moved up to Blood Warrior's side growling, "The baby-killing bitch is mine!" Blood Warrior chuckled as he looked at Delilah, "I wouldn't be you right now for all the deer in our territory! I would rather fight this monster you call a mate than Tasha defending her pups!"

Blood Warrior saw the flash of fear in Red Fang's eyes. Red Fang backpedaled a few steps, leaving Delilah in front. Red Fang grinned, "Okay Blood Warrior, you have certainly taught me a lesson. I will leave here today a better and wiser wolf. I think under different circumstances we could really be good friends." Red Fang submissively drew closer to Blood Warrior as he whined, "I am truly sorry for my actions. The truth is my father and mother were not good wolves. They raised me wrong. But you have shown me the error of my ways. From this day forward, I am a changed wolf!"

Red Fang had moved within striking distance of Blood Warrior but his problem was the reduced distance also put him within range of Blood Warrior.

Barky shouted, "Watch that son of a bitch! Don't trust him!"

A small echo squeaked, "Son of a bitch."

Quicker than a rattlesnake strike, Blood Warrior snapped at Red Fang's face. One of his fangs ripped out one of Red Fang's eyes. The eye dangled by a blood soaked thread from its socket. Blood Warrior then attacked Red Fang's exposed throat, sinking his teeth into it.

Blood Warrior shook him like a meadowlark would shake a worm. Blood Warrior was not sadistic. He killed to eat and to defend his family. That was the way of the animal kingdom. But the thoughts of all his family that Red Fang killed or had ordered killed made Blood Warrior want to prolong his death and suffering.

Red Fang pleaded for his life, whining, "Please, please, please, don't kill me. I will do anything. I can be a big help to you."

Blood Warrior turned Red Fang loose and growled, "There is only one thing you can do for me."

Red Fang groveled, "Anything! You name it! You got it!"

Blood Warrior snarled, "What you can do for me is… *DIE!*"

Blood Warrior grabbed Red Fang by the neck and choked the life from him with his powerful jaws. Blood Warrior threw Red Fang's body off to the side in disgust. The still body thudded up against the trunk of a massive pine tree. Red Fang was now the property of the forest scavengers.

During the brief fight between Blood Warrior and Red Fang, Delilah attacked Tasha. But Tasha was too fast for her, dodging her charge and latching onto her neck as she went by. As Delilah thrashed around trying to shake Tasha's hold on her neck, Delilah was attacked by the two alpha females from the consolidated pack. The three females made short work of the evil Delilah.

When she was dead, the first alpha female barked to Tasha, "I know you didn't need any help handling the likes of her but I couldn't help myself. I've wanted to sink my teeth into her from the first time I saw her."

The other alpha female seconded that feeling. "I consider it an honor to play even a small part in ending the life of that vile degenerate."

After spending the next week together in a loose pack, Blood Warrior called all the wolves together for a meeting. "We actually have three packs here. The three packs need to stay separate to follow the laws of Father Wolf. Each of the other two packs should select a new leader from the opposite pack. That way the litters are not inbred and become a foul pack like Red Fang's."

The alpha female for the first pack barked, "First, we want to thank you, Blood Warrior, for ridding us of that cursed scourge, Red Fang! Second, I want to ask Valor something." She turned to Valor, "Would you be my mate and the leader of our pack?"

Valor looked at Blood Warrior and Tasha. They both nodded their heads in agreement. Valor faced his new mate, "I pledge my loyalty and courage to you and our pack!"

The alpha female from the second pack tapped the oldest male from the first pack as her new mate and pack leader.

The next day, the other two packs left to go establish their own territories to raise their own families. When it was time for Valor to leave, he licked each of the black pups and shyly licked Blood Warrior and Tasha. Tasha had tears leaking from her eyes.

Valor barked, "I don't know where to start. I owe you two so much. It seems like a lifetime ago that you had the bad luck to meet a wolf called Dolt..."

Blood Warrior quickly cut him off. "I have no idea what you're talking about. I vaguely remember some wolf by that name but he died a long time ago. Don't ever mention his name again. It's bad luck to speak about the dead."

Valor looked up in the trees at the squirrels. "Goodbye, old friends. You have also taught me a lot!"

Barky chattered, "It is an honor to be your friend. I will always be your friend!" Missy could not say anything as tears streamed down her face.

The two packs departed for their new homes. Valor and his pack went to the left. The other pack went to the right.

After all the conflict and bloodshed, Blood Warrior ,Tasha and their children, and Barky, Missy and their children all settled in for an uneventful life filled with peace. Unfortunately, life doesn't always cooperate.

The crows descended on the body of Red Fang, eager to treat themselves to an easy meal. They inched up to Red Fang, wanting to make sure he was really dead. The bravest crow speared Red Fang's dangling eye. When he jerked the eyeball away, popping the attached string, Red Fang's eyelid rolled open, revealing the bloody pit that once held the eye. This startled the crow, who hopped backwards with a sharp caw, the eyeball still stuck on his beak.

The crows nervously moved away from Red Fang as his second eye burst open. Red Fang gingerly lifted his head, causing the flock of crows to abandon their hoped-for feast with raucous protests, winging their way to the safety of the trees.

Red Fang could see with his one eye that a crow was sitting on an Aspen limb eating his other eye. Red Fang's breathing had been so shallow that it had been undetectable. Now his lungs began to fill with deeper breaths. He lay for over an hour, recovering, before he hobbled off. Red Fang scarcely noticed the body of Delilah. He did not care about her in life, in death even less so.

As he made his escape, Red Fang thought, *Blood Warrior thinks he's seen the last of me. He will see the deaths of each of his family members before I kill him. He will pay for everything he's done to me, including the loss of my eye. I will also wipe out that damn squirrel family. And, I was way too easy on my traitorous pack. They took advantage of my good nature, but they will pay dearly for their treachery. They all think I am finished, but I am just getting started. Red Fang is dead, but One Eye has been born and his vengeance will be terrible to behold.*

ACKNOWLEDGEMENTS

I am grateful for the constant support of my wife, Tina, and my children: Jacob, Caleb, Sarah and Ainslee.

Thank you to Missy Brewer for editing this book, to Michael Campbell for the book design, and to Bryan Gehrke for the cover artwork.

William Joiner can be contacted at bridgetexas@yahoo.com

Learn more at
www.williamjoinerauthor.com

Joining the Rewards Club on my website is 100% FREE and scores you a FREE eBook copy of *American Entrepreneur*. As a Rewards Club member you will receive monthly notices of future give-a-ways and special promotions. My pledge to you is you won't receive an email from me more than once a month.

www.williamjoinerauthor.com